Praise for

"As a blind child, I really enjoy information about blind people and what they do. I also loved the characters and the plot. I thought it was very suspenseful. A great read for the sighted or blind. I would highly recommend it."

- Layla Hildenbrand, age ten, two-time National Braille Challenge Finalist

"As the parent of a blind child, I absolutely adored reading *Just Maria*. Blindness is not a tragedy and does not limit one's ability. Jay Hardwig brilliantly gave us a character that proves such. Maria is like any other child who makes some bad decisions, struggles with friendships, and ultimately proves her independence despite being blind. I highly recommend this book to all readers…tweens, teens, adults, blind or sighted."

- Stacey Hildenbrand, Layla's mom and a certified teacher for the visually impaired

"At the heart of Jay Hardwig's *Just Maria* is the wickedly funny Maria Romero, a blind twelve-year-old heroine who is both exceptional…and normal. While physically challenged to navigate crowded school halls and busy streets, she must also find her way through the usual emotional labyrinth of popularity, friendships, and independence. Visually impaired readers will, for once, see themselves at the center of a story. Sighted readers will be treated to a vivid portrayal of how a blind kid sees the world. Most importantly, though, Hardwig's nuanced, witty novel celebrates how all of us, sighted or not, must look inward to see true friendship, character, and courage. After putting this book down I felt as if I could accomplish anything."

- Allan Wolf, author of *The Watch that Ends the Night* and *The Snow Fell Three Graves Deep*

JUST MARIA

Jay Hardwig

Fitzroy Books

Published by Fitzroy Books
An imprint of
Regal House Publishing, LLC
Raleigh, NC 27612
All rights reserved

https://fitzroybooks.com

Printed in the United States of America

ISBN -13 (paperback): 9781646030828
ISBN -13 (epub): 9781646031078
Library of Congress Control Number: 781646030828

Interior and cover design by Lafayette & Greene
Cover images © by C.B. Royal

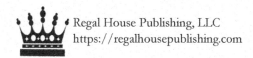

Regal House Publishing, LLC
https://regalhousepublishing.com

Printed in the United States of America

To Nita: pathfinder, cloudlifter, hiking buddy.

CONTENTS

1

Undies

My friend Sam—he's blind, like me—says that to tell his dirty undies from his clean, he has to sniff 'em.

That's gross, I tell him.

He shrugs.

That's why you put your cleans in one place and your dirties in another, I tell him. You'll never have to sniff 'em again.

Too much work, he says.

Too much work? That's crazy, I tell him. That's lazy.

He shrugs again. You do it your way, and I'll do it mine, he says.

Fair enough. But there's one thing I know: it's not too much work for me. I want things in their place, so I can find them, every time. I want my things to have a *where*.

And I don't just want a *where*, but a *how* and a *why* too. What makes things go? What makes them stay? What makes the circle round, the trumpet sound, the toast get brown? The way I see it, things have an order, a rhyme, a reason, and if I can find it out, I will. Mom says I'm her little scientist, but I don't see why that makes me a scientist. Given a choice between a guess and an answer, I'd rather have the answer.

Wouldn't you?

Wouldn't Sam?

I can't speak for Sam, but I'll tell you this: I know where my cleans are.

2

Not Magic

People think that because I'm blind I must be magic. Like I'm some amazing creature from a faraway planet. Some kind of savant, or a robot, or a robot savant. People think my hearing is so sharp I can hear a pin drop from around the corner, or a baby robin crack its egg from three blocks away. I can't.

Or maybe they think I have a super sense of feeling. Like with my fingertips alone, I can feel the color of a feather or the age of stone. I can't.

My ears and fingers work just the same as yours. If I hear more, it's because I listen. If I feel more, it's because I pay attention.

You see? No superpowers. I use what I've got to make sense of this world, same as you do. I'm not incredible. I'm not amazing. I'm just a girl. A girl who was born with tumors in her eyes.

That's why it bugged me so much when JJ Munson came over yesterday with all this superhero detective agency garbage. Yes, him. The celebrated JJ Munson, King Geek of the Sixth Grade. I'm the girl who's lucky enough to live just down the street from JJ Munson. I've known him since third grade, when his family moved onto the block, but I wouldn't exactly call us friends. In fact, I wouldn't even come close.

JJ's one of those weird kids, a bit of a spaz, with a mind all over the place. Oh sure, he's nice enough, smart in his own way, but he says the weirdest things. Once he told Mr. Smith that he'd glued his ear to his shoulder. He spent twenty straight minutes with his head cocked to the side, trying to sell the joke, even though we all figured out in ten seconds flat that it wasn't true. Another time he asked Mrs. Newton if fish fart. I mean really. And once he spent all of math class pretending his protractor was a secret portal to a hidden world, a fifth dimension that was guarded by a half-dog, half-man named Walter. *(Walter!)* So he's that kind of kid.

My friends call him all sorts of things, most of which I won't repeat here, but let's just say that *paste-eater* might be about the nicest thing.

So, when he came over to the house all excited, just bursting at the seams, I knew to take it with a grain of salt. Truth told, I was annoyed he came. I was home alone. I don't get to be home alone much, and I was determined to enjoy it. I was sitting on the couch, doing nothing, exactly nothing, which was exactly what I wanted to be doing, when I heard footsteps coming up our driveway.

I knew it was JJ before he even knocked on the door. First there was the heavy thud of his big boots on our wood porch, then his wet rasping wheeze through the window. Next came the familiar rhythmic knock—*shave and a haircut, two bits*—and the impatient shuffle as he shifted from foot to foot.

I opened the door.

"Hey, Maria, it's JJ," he breathed.

I knew that already, but at least he said it. You'd be amazed at how many people just stand there, waiting for me to guess who they are. Worse are the ones who coo, "Can you guess whose voice this is?" I get that all the time. Like I'm a carnival act. The tic-tac-toe-playing chicken at the county fair. The *Who is This?* game definitely makes my Crabby-Abby Days Top Ten List of the Most Annoying Things About Being Blind.

So I appreciate that JJ bothers to say his name, because who knows? Maybe someday another fat kid with asthma and army boots will move in down the block, with the same syncopated door knock, and then I'll have trouble telling them apart. (Except that JJ always smells like yellow mustard. I don't know why. But he does.)

Anyway, he came busting in with news of his latest harebrained scheme. Harebrained schemes from JJ are nothing new, and sometimes I like to just stick around to see how far from the Ferris wheel JJ's brain has flung him this time.

He had barely caught his breath before he said, "I want you to be my partner."

"Your partner?" I flinched. "In what?"

He threw his hands across the air, as if imagining a sign lit up like the Fourth of July. I only know this because the next thing he said was, "I'm throwing my hands across the air, Maria, as if I'm imagining a sign lit up like the Fourth of July."

He stretched his arms out wide—he told me this too—and paused magnificently.

"The Twinnoggin Superhero Detective Agency!" he pronounced.

"Twinnoggin?"

"Yeah," he said. "Cool, isn't it? *Twinnoggin*. Like twin noggins. Two heads. You and me. Me and you. It's either that or Wonder Twins."

"Stick with Twinnoggin," I said.

"So you're in?"

"I didn't say that."

Superhero Detective Agency? I thought. *What is this, some kind of children's show?* I mean, I loved *Nate the Great*, too, but that was five years ago. I tried to show the doubt on my face. Ms. Nita tells me that sighted kids do it all the time—show their feelings on their faces, without using any words—so I did my best to make my face show doubt. (Ms. Nita says that doubt looks like wrinkled eyebrows and a pouty mouth.) But I guess it didn't work, because JJ barreled straight ahead.

5

"It'll be great. A real-life detective agency, the two of us playing to our greatest strengths. The way I see it, I'm the brains of the outfit. I've done a lot of reading, watched all the shows. I can sift the evidence, see the angles, figure out how the puzzle fits together."

"I see," I said.

"And you? You've got something special. That intuition. A sixth sense. I don't know, I can't explain it. Maybe it's ESP. But you know things before they even happen. It's like you're on some different wavelength."

Intuition? A different wavelength? I'd hoped for better from him. But I humored him just the same. "What kind of cases would we solve?"

"We'd have to start small at first," he said. "Petty crimes." You could tell by his voice how excited he was. "Probably just things around the school. Like who's writing on the bathroom walls."

"Someone's writing on the bathroom walls?" I asked. Funny. I hadn't noticed.

"Yeah, it's all over the boys' room. I hear there's some in the girls' room too."

"What does it say?"

"I can't repeat it," JJ said. "Let's just say that someone doesn't take a fond view of Mr. Zukowski." Mr. Zukowski is our principal. He's strict, that's for sure, and has this no-nonsense voice that makes you feel like you're always either in trouble or right on the edge of it. The kids in my school like to pretend they aren't scared of anything, but a good half of them are scared of Mr. Zukowski.

"Whoever it is, they need to learn to spell," JJ added. I didn't ask for details.

"That's the first I've heard of it," I say.

"Yeah, well…"

It should be pretty obvious to you by now that I don't see writing. You can write it on the board, write it on the walls, write it outside the school in ten-foot-high neon letters—it's all the same to me. All those papers they pass out every day in school? They mean nothing to me. My friend Sam calls them UPOs: Unidentified Paper Objects. The world is full of them. Ms. Nita—she's the teacher who taught me braille—says that a smartphone can read all those papers to me, but I can't use one in school, not yet, so for now I can't do much with those papers except make airplanes. Either that or ask someone with good eyes what they say. So, if something was written on the walls in the girls' bathroom, I'd have to ask Chloe what it said, at least if I wanted to keep up with the life and times of Marble City Middle.

"Okay," I told JJ. "There's writing on the bathroom walls. That's not much to build a detective agency on. What else you got?"

"Who was Tommy Treadwell kissing in the stairwell when he got busted by Zukowski?"

"Like I care."

"What's *really* in the door marked Broom Closet?"

"Brooms?" I said.

"I'm guessing more than brooms," JJ replied. "And what's *really* in the Sloppy Joes they serve in the lunchroom?"

"Burning questions," I said.

"I know, right?" he said. "I mean, is it more, or less, than ten percent roadkill? It's a mystery *and* a math problem."

"JJ—"

"Like I said, we'll have to start small. But who knows where it'll end up? The sky's the limit."

There was no use arguing with him. I shrugged, but kept quiet.

"Well," said JJ, "I better scram. I'm watching Cynthia, and *Clifford The Big Red Dog* is almost over. She'll be on the move soon."

I saw him to the door. Just before clodhopping down our front stairs, JJ paused.

"Think about it," he said.

"I will," I lied.

"Just imagine," he said, "with my smarts and your magic, we'll be a perfect pair."

If that's what he thinks, we're doomed.

Because he's not smart.

And I'm not magic.

3

My Crabby-Abby Days Top Ten List of the Most

Annoying Things About Being Blind,

In No Particular Order,

Numbers 1-3

Don't get me wrong. I'm fine with being blind. I better be, because I don't have a choice, but the truth is, I wouldn't change it, not even if I could. Blind is part of who I am, and I'm proud of who I am.

Still, I have my crabby days. Sam says just because I'm blind doesn't mean I can't be a crabby crank every once in a while, and I agree. So Sam and I decided to call them my Crabby-Abby Days, and then we came up with My Crabby-Abby Days Top Ten List of the Most Annoying Things About Being Blind, In No Particular Order. Here are three of them:

1. The "Can you guess who this is?" game
2. UPOs (Unidentified Paper Objects)
3. People who think I'm amazing

More on that later.

I suppose I should tell you something else about Sam: he doesn't live here. Not anywhere near here. He lives in Dallas, Texas, which is about a thousand miles away from here. I've met him exactly once, at some Blind Kid Conference our moms went to, and we hit it off. It took less than forty-eight hours for Sam to become my best friend, which tells you two things: 1) Sam is a cool kid; 2) I don't have many friends. When the conference was over, we promised to stay in touch, and we have. We talk on the phone, chat online, and text almost every day. We compare notes about what it's like to be blind in a world where most everyone can see. He's a good friend with a good heart. But he's awful far away.

4

Home Alone

Just as the sound of JJ's army boots clomping down the front steps faded into the distance, I heard Mom's car in the driveway. I waited for the crisp clip-clop of her dress shoes on the wooden steps, and was surprised to hear the muffled squeak of sneakers instead.

That meant she had gone to the gym after work—no big deal for most moms, but a big deal for mine. It was only three months ago that she dared to leave me home alone for the first time. For five minutes. To run to the store for her headache powders.

For all the planning and worry that went into that trip, you'd have thought she was organizing the Winter Olympics. She made me recite three different emergency phone numbers and placed a cellphone right in my hand, as if I couldn't be trusted to find it on the table in case I needed it. It's like she was afraid I would start a small kitchen fire, self-combust, or maybe just evaporate. Or what if the zombie apocalypse started and she wasn't around to protect me? So, yeah, she went a little overboard, but I guess I can understand. It was the first time she'd left her blind baby daughter alone in the house.

(Let me remind you I'm twelve years old.)

I wasn't worried. I just sat there and enjoyed the experience, all alone in the house for the first time. But Mom told me her heart was in her throat the whole time she was down at the Quik-Stop. Since then, she'd tried it twice more, a little longer each time. I encouraged her, told her I was fine, really. How could she see her friends if she couldn't leave me alone, not even for a minute? Or find a new boyfriend for that matter? And what did she think would happen after high school? Was she planning to move into my college dorm too? How could she expect to have a life if I was always by her side? How could I? Mom says she doesn't need a life as long as she has me. She says that I am all she needs. But I know that can't last, not for me and not for her. Sooner or later, she's going to have to let me grow up a little. By my accounting, she's running about two years behind schedule. So when I heard her gym shoes on the front porch, I was happy.

Her gym shoes meant that, after working up the courage to leave me alone for five minutes, then ten, then fifteen, she was now able to leave me alone for almost an hour. Today was just the second time she'd allowed herself to go to the gym after work. The first time, she'd come home an absolute wreck.

"That one spin class," she told me, after giving me the biggest hug in the history of big hugs, "was bought at the price of forty-five minutes of gut-wrenching worry."

"I was fine, Mom."

"Gut-wrenching worry might be good for my abs, but it's terrible for the lines around my eyes."

"Stop it."

"No really. Feel them. I think they're a half-inch deeper than they were this morning."

I felt her face. The wrinkles around her eyes—I've always loved them—felt like they always did. "Nope. Not any deeper," I said.

"Are you kidding?" my mom laughed. "I think I could lose my keys in there."

"Well, I wasn't going to say anything," I told her. "But I did find two nickels and a dime."

"Very funny."

"Don't worry, Mom. You're beautiful." That may sound

like faint praise coming from a blind girl, but deep down, Mom knew I was right. I did too.

It was a nice moment, but not one I cared to repeat. It couldn't be a big production every time she left me alone, or every time she came back and found me still alive. So this time, when I heard Mom's sneakers on the front door, I decided not to mention it, not to even let on that I noticed she'd been gone. That would bring us one step closer to normal.

Mom must have felt the same way, because she played it just a bit *too* carefree when she came in the door. No hugs, no talk about the lines around her eyes. She even made a point of whistling a little tune—*tweedle-dee, tweedle-dee, I'm just a bird on a branch*—which was a dead giveaway. When I hear my mom whistling, I know something's the matter and she's trying to act like it isn't. She whistled a lot in the months before Dad left.

"What did JJ want?" she asked, her voice bright but a little forced. "He seemed excited."

"He's got some crazy club he wants me to join."

"What kind of club?"

"I think it's a detective agency," I said.

"A detective agency?"

"Yeah, you know, to solve all those pressing middle school crimes. I think he's calling it the *Double Dork Superdumb Detective Agency.*"

"Be nice."

"I was," I said.

"I doubt it," Mom said.

"But—"

"You may have acted nice. But acting nice and being nice are two different things."

"I know."

"*Acting nice* is when you're with him. *Being nice* is even after he's gone."

"He's such a weirdo, Mom."

"He's our neighbor," Mom said. "And our friend."

"Your friend, maybe."

"Maria, we've talked about this. I just think you could make more of an effort."

"What? You want the two of us freaks together?"

"Honey—"

"The Fabulous Franklin Avenue Freak Show," I snorted. "We'll be the most popular kids in the whole school."

"Hush," Mom said.

She was right, of course, but I couldn't help myself.

"Maria," she said. "I would think you, of all people, would—"

"All right already!" I interrupted. I know how that sentence ends. *I would think you, of all people, would know what it's like to be different.* And that's just the problem. I do understand what it's like. And I understand that it's hard enough for a *girl like me* to find friends without having a mouth-breather like JJ Munson shackled to my leg, with his army boots and his asthma and his superhero crime-solving club. No thanks.

This is usually about the time in the conversation when Mom plays the Cynthia card.

"His life's not so easy either, you know," Mom said.

Bingo. Right on cue. This conversation would be a lot more interesting if I hadn't had it a million times before.

"Think about Cynthia," she said. "He's got a lot of responsibility for a boy his age."

I'm three steps ahead of you, Mom, I think, but I don't say it.

Cynthia is JJ's little sister. She's severely autistic. Like the kind that doesn't talk, and can't take care of herself. I've met her a few times. She seems nice enough, but what do I know? Since she can't talk, and I can't see, I don't have much to go on.

I've got to admit, though: JJ's great with her. He watches her every day after school. Gets her a snack, helps her find her favorite TV show. Makes sure she's safe and happy. She doesn't act out, JJ tells me, but she does need constant supervision. I guess to make sure she doesn't wander out of the house or stick a fork in the toaster or anything like that. Mom talks like Cynthia's a burden to her family, but JJ never acts that way. He loves her to pieces. I could tell he'd do anything for her. I bet her mom would too.

Of course, JJ's mom probably thinks *we* have it hard. A single mom with a blind girl. A blind girl whose Dad skipped town seven years ago. I'll agree: it does sound kind of bad when you put it like that. But it's not like he was much help even when he was here.

It's not a perfect life, but then, whose is? I know I wouldn't trade it. And I suppose the Munsons wouldn't trade theirs either. Whether that's wisdom or just pride, I don't know. But I do know this: we're not wasting much time feeling sorry for ourselves.

5

Things You Might Be Wondering, Part One:
How I Went Blind

I'm guessing you have some questions, and that's okay. Everyone does. Maybe I'm the first blind person you've ever read about, or ever even thought about. And now you have questions, but it feels a little awkward.

Don't worry.

I'm here to help.

I'll do my best to answer the questions you already have but are afraid to ask.

I'm nice that way.

The first question I usually get is how I went blind. I've already told you I was born with tumors in my eyes. By that I mean eye cancer. The doctors call it *retinoblastoma*, because the tumors started in the part of my eyes called the retina, which is the thin little layer of cells in the back of your eyes that responds to light. Mom says that the retina captures all the images that come in through our eyes, and sends those images back to the brain for processing. And like any other part of your body, the retina is made up of millions and bajillions of cells. My problem was that my retinas grew too many cells. They didn't stop once they filled up the retina. They just kept on growing, making not just my retinas but the tumors that blinded me too.

The doctor says I could probably see a little bit when I was born, but if so, I never learned to make much sense of it. I don't remember it anyway. The tumors were aggressive. The doctors had hoped they could treat them, or at least save one of my eyes, but it didn't work out that way. I was ten months old when they took my right eye. Three months later, they took my left. And when I say *took*, I mean it: they plucked those suckers right out of there. My mom says they were worried the tumors would spread, from my eyes to my brain. Once my eyes stopped working, it was an easy choice, she says. They didn't just take the eyes. They took the cancer.

In their place, I got glass eyeballs. Not only do they make it look like I've got eyes—at least if you're not paying close attention—but they also keep my face in line. The doctor says if I had empty eye sockets, there's a chance that the tissues around them would grow weak and shrink. Like my face would cave in, a little. The glass eyes keep those eye sockets nice and round and normal-looking. At least that's what they tell me.

So the eyes that you see when you look at me are fakes. They're not actually glass, either, but a kind of plastic that looks like glass. And they're shaped like shells more than balls. I can take them out if I want to—that's a good trick for freaking out the lunchroom—but Mom says I need to keep them in, and not to be playing around with them. It's not many moms who get to say, *Put your eyeballs in, dear. Company's coming*. But mine does.

You can order your fake eyes in all sorts of colors these days. I told Mom I wanted one pink and one purple. She said maybe in college. For now my choices are hazel, brown, and blue. Someone told me once that even blind kids want blue eyes. Not me. Mine are brown, deep brown. Like pools of chocolate you could dive right into. I'm told they're beautiful.

6

More Weirdness from JJ

Okay. Your turn. When I got home from school the next day, there was someone on my porch: army boots, wet wheeze, mustard. Who was it?

Did you say JJ Munson?

Congratulations! You are 100 percent right! I didn't say one word about what he looked like, either.

You see? It's not that hard being blind.

So get over me already.

Done?

Done.

So, yeah, JJ Munson was on my porch when I got home from school. Did I invite him in? No, I did not. I kept him on the porch. Because once JJ gets inside, there's no telling when he'll leave. Plus Mom was in the kitchen, and I didn't want her listening in. Because once Mom starts listening in, she starts pulling the puppet strings, making things happen, running the show. There's always something I could be doing better: asking questions, facing the speaker, standing *just the right distance* away. I know she's just trying to help, but sometimes it gets old. Exhausting, even.

And then, of course, she'll tell me I've got to be nice and make friends. I mean, I'm all for being nice and making friends, but I think I get to choose when to be nice, and who to make friends with. And JJ's not on that list.

"So what's up, JJ?" I asked, after he'd settled his big solid self into one of the chairs on our porch.

"Captain Munson," he said. "The preferred term is Captain Munson."

"O...kay," I said. "Got it. So what's up...JJ?"

He paused. "It might interest you to know that I'm here with the latest dispatch from the Twinnogin World Headquarters."

"Or it might not," I said.

"I see the young Maria is in a combative mood," JJ said. "A bit peevish, it seems."

"*Peevish?*"

"Feisty. Let me be the first to admit that I was a little rash yesterday, when I proposed we form the Twinnogin Detective Agency."

"Well, actually, JJ, I'm glad to hear that because—"

"To imagine that we could just create our own detective agency, as easy as snapping our fingers." He snapped his fingers. "Just like that."

"I know what you mean. I thought it was a bit ridic—"

"Detective is not a title one can simply *claim*," he continued. "Detective is a title that is earned, not given. Why, at this moment, Maria, we are no more detectives than we are astronauts."

"Or pastry chefs," I said.

"Or pastry chefs," he conceded.

"Or dolphin trainers," I added. "We are neither detectives, nor pastry chefs, nor dolphin trainers. We are sixth-grade kids at Marble City Middle."

"Agreed," JJ said. "We are rank amateurs. Which is why we must *prove* ourselves worthy of the title *detective*."

"Pardon?"

"I propose a series of challenges." He inhaled deeply, and I braced myself for some serious blather. "A series of challenges that shall test both our minds and our mettle, to determine if we have what it truly takes to be detectives." His voice took on a heroic cast. "Like Odysseus and Aeneas before us, we must run the gauntlet of affliction and prove ourselves brave in the face of peril, wise in the midst of folly, and above all, loyal, good, and true. We shall be guardians of honor, heroes in a fallen age."

You sound a little nuts, I thought.

"The challenges shall be four," he intoned.

Maybe more than a little.

"Do not think, dear Maria, that these challenges are yours alone. No, I must earn the title too. The process is simple: I shall set your challenges, and you set mine. You give me the first challenge, and after I have faced it, and tasted either success or failure, I shall challenge you. Following that, you challenge me again. Whether we are bathed in glory or cloaked in blackest shame, we persevere. And so it shall continue, back and forth, forth and back, you and I, the two of us, until we each have faced four challenges, and discovered whether we have the stuff—the valor, the virtue, the grit—to be true heroes."

"Honey, who are you talking to?" Mom yelled from indoors.

Sometimes I'm not sure, I thought.

"It's JJ," I hollered back.

"Oh, JJ! How nice! I'll come out and join you two."

"No, that's okay," I said. "He's got to be going anyway."

"I do?" JJ asked.

"The time." I pressed the speech button on my talking watch. *It's three fifty-six p.m.,* the watch blared.

"Ah yes," JJ said. "The end of *Clifford* is nigh. Duty awaits. But I am so glad we had this conversation, Maria. I look forward to this noble and invigorating quest. May fortune favor the bold. In the meantime, I await your initial challenge. I have no doubt that it will be sublime."

"You are such a weirdo," I hissed. I could hear my mom walking towards the door. "Why can't you be normal for just one day?"

He drew in his breath, as if to reply, but just then my mom opened the door.

"Why, JJ, so good to see you," my mom said.

"And you, too, Miss Romero."

"I was just about to invite you in," Mom said. "Is it true you have to go?"

"That I do, Miss Romero. Cynthia awaits. But it's been a most auspicious day, don't you think?"

"I suppose it has," Mom said.

"Now, I must take my leave. I bid you a most magical and magnificent farewell." He trundled off the porch and up the walk.

We stood there a moment. I waited until his footfalls had faded away and I could be sure he was well gone.

"See what I mean?" I whispered to my mom.

"Hush," she said, and led me indoors.

7

Things You Might Be Wondering, Part Two: Braille

The second thing you're probably wondering about is braille. I get a lot of questions about braille. Yeah, I read braille. It's just a bunch of bumps on a page—lots and lots of tiny dots—all arranged by one big crazy code. And, yeah, I read it with my fingers. I've gotten pretty good too. My fingers can fly across those dots, though not as fast as some kids I know. So it's cool, yeah, super-great, amazing. I get that. But I sure am glad I didn't have to learn to read print. I mean, think about it. I read with my fingers. You read *with your eyes*. That's what's amazing to me. You make sense of all these tiny little squiggles that stand for letters—*a, j, k, y, z*—hundreds of them on every page, all crammed together to form words. And you can't even feel them to make sure of what you're seeing. I don't know how you do it.

I mean, I bet right now, your eyeballs are flying over these little letters. Super-fast. Gliding along, line by line, and your brain is telling you what all these little squiggles mean, turning them into words, one right after another, *bang bang bang*, until you've got sentences and paragraphs and chapters and whole stories, all laid out in tiny little squiggles. You've done it so many times by now you don't even notice it, but back when you were first learning to read, I bet it was hard to tell the shapes apart, one squiggle from another. But you practiced and practiced, and slowly got better, and now you don't even think about it. Well, it's the same for me. Except I use fingers on dots, not eyes on print. It's not that hard.

You'd learn it too, if you were blind.

8

Hannah and The Others

So I haven't told you about Hannah Anderson yet. She's only the most popular girl in the whole school. Cheerleader, teacher's pet, all the boys have a crush on her, that sort of thing. She knows it. And she knows that you know it too.

My friend Chloe says that Hannah doesn't have time for anyone less beautiful than her, but if that's true, Hannah wouldn't have time for anyone. Because as far as I can tell, Hannah thinks she's the most beautiful girl in the school, except maybe her best friend Kaitlyn. But I bet Hannah thinks Kaitlyn isn't more than eighty percent as pretty as her. Maybe ninety on a good day.

Plus Hannah's two-faced. She's all sweet to me, probably because she thinks *helping the blind girl* will look good on her college application. When teachers are around, she's always eager to help me. Help me do this, help me do that. It's mostly help I don't need.

But I've seen Hannah when the teachers aren't around. I hear her say the worst things about other girls. I wonder what she says about me, when I'm not around.

So you would think that I wouldn't want anything to do with Hannah, right? She's a two-faced stuck-up princess, who's only nice when she feels like it.

That's just the problem. I *do* want her to like me. I *want* to be in her group, with Kaitlyn and Jasmine and all the rest. To be cool and popular and all that, have friends at every lunch table. I mean, I don't expect to be a queen bee or anything, but I'd at least like to be a part of the hive.

Is that so wrong?

I already told you Hannah can be mean. And when she's mean, she's really mean, and then I don't want anything to do with her. But she can also be nice, and when she's nice—or at least nice to me—then it's *exactly what I want*. I want to be her best friend, if only for the day.

And I don't even know if she likes me, likes me for real, or just pities me.

It's maddening.

One thing I know for sure, though, is you can't afford to get Hannah on your bad side. If she decides you're *not cool*, a dork, a loser, a lame-brain, whatever word she's using that day, then your chances of ever being anybody are just about done at Marble City Middle. It happened to Ruby. It happened to Ariana. It could happen to me.

So mostly when I'm around Hannah, I try to play it cool. Nothing too different, nothing too weird. I hold my chin up, turn towards whoever's talking, try not to call attention to myself. And when JJ Munson's name comes up, I *definitely* shut up. I don't want them knowing he's been anywhere near my front porch.

Which is why my gut did a few backflips the next morning when I heard Hannah say, "Look at Munson today!"

"Whoa," said Kaitlyn.

"What happened to him?" Jasmine asked.

"Looks like he finally found a comb," said Hannah.

"Maybe the social worker gave him one," snickered Kaitlyn.

"And a decent shirt too," said Jasmine.

"How long until he gets a ketchup stain on it?" asked Hannah.

"Two days," guessed Kaitlyn.

"More like two hours," I said. The girls laughed.

"Here he comes!" squealed Jasmine. I winced. What if he said something about the Twinnoggin Detective Agency? Right here, in front of my friends? I could just see him going on about honor and Odysseus and all that crazy mouth-breathing talk of his. I would absolutely die.

"Hello, Munson," said Hannah.

"Good morning," he said. He inhaled wetly. I was sure he was about to say something more.

This was it. This was the moment I dreaded. If it wasn't something about the detective agency, it was going to be something about dwarves. Or time travel. Or time-traveling dwarves. Or worse, something about me. *Dwarves are fine*, I thought. *Just please please don't say anything about me.*

And he didn't. He inhaled, then exhaled, then just kept on walking, up to the teacher's desk to turn in his homework. I couldn't believe it. I couldn't remember the last time JJ had kept his big fat weird mouth shut. But I was sure glad he did it this time.

I wasn't the only one who noticed. "That's odd," Hannah said as he left. "Maybe that social worker gave him a brain too."

"I doubt it," I said. My face flushed when I said it, but when I heard the girls laughing, I added, "It's hard to find a brain that fits an overgrown tree slug."

"Tree slug!" Kaitlyn crowed.

"Get the salt," Jasmine said.

"Girl, you crack me up," said Hannah. "You should hang out with us more."

I felt bad, it's true, talking about JJ that way.

But when they laughed? I won't deny it.

That felt good.

I didn't see JJ for the rest of the day.

And, yes, I know I used the word *see* there. It's okay. Blind people use all the same words you do, and that's okay. It's okay to ask me, *See what I mean?* when we're talking, or to tell me to *take a look at this* when there's something cool you want me to check out. I'll do the same to you.

So, when I say I didn't see JJ for the rest of the day, of course I didn't see him. I'm blind. But I also didn't hear him, smell him, sense him, catch wind of him, stumble over his big stinking feet, or get drawn into his orbit in any way. That's what I meant when I said I didn't see him. And you know what? I'm glad I didn't.

It's true: the celebrated JJ Munson kept to himself and stayed quiet. There were no oddball questions to the teacher, no rambling on about his pet spiders or the properties of banana milkshakes in zero gravity rocket boosters. During lunch—which, as usual, he ate by himself—I heard none of his usual blabber, no praise-songs for King Potato and his Gravy Navy. It was a day of blessed quiet.

He didn't drop by after school either, to ask about his challenge or update me on the latest gumshoe intrigue. I wondered if maybe he was upset at me, if maybe he'd heard what I'd said to Hannah and her friends. But he couldn't have, not from the teacher's desk. He was too far away. Maybe something came up with Cynthia, or maybe he was just feeling a little down. Truth is, I didn't question it too much. I was just glad for the break.

But if there's one thing I know about breaks like that? They don't last.

9

Zig-Zag

Sure enough, the next morning, before we even went to school, JJ was on my doorstep, as fresh and nutty as ever, knocking out his tell-tale rhythm on the doorframe. If I thought I was off the Munson Train, I thought wrong.

"How about that!" JJ crowed, just as soon as I poked my head out the screen door.

"How about what?" I grumbled.

"My first test!" he cried. "A victory for Captain Munson!"

"What are you talking about?"

"It was a clever challenge, Maria. Fiendish, even. I was surprised at first, I'll admit it. I had anticipated something more *physical*. Scaling a smooth wall. Racing a greyhound. Threading a needle whilst wearing boxing gloves."

Whilst? What century is this?

"But then I thought, *of course not!* For Maria Romero understands that the gifts of the detective are the gifts of disguise. Disguise and misdirection are the name of the game. Being that which you are not. Real cloak-and-dagger stuff."

"What on earth are you talking about, JJ?"

"And so I thought to myself: I shall take a page from Maria's playbook, and issue a similar challenge. To be a chameleon, a contradiction, a riddle. To zig where others zag. Keep 'em on their toes."

"JJ, the bus will be here any minute. I've got to—"

"Ah, yes. Our Maria is a prompt one. Direct. Candid. A straight shooter. Another mark in her favor."

"JJ, what are you—"

"Just tell me, Maria. Did I pass the test?"

"What test?"

"My first challenge."

"What challenge?"

"The one you issued as I left your house, not thirty-six hours ago. Surely you remember."

"Surely I don't."

"Surely you do. You said, 'Can't you be normal, for just one day?' And I did it! I completely and utterly did it! I was normal—so, so normal—all day yesterday!"

Oh dear god, I thought.

"I won't pretend it wasn't difficult. I don't see how you people do it, really. But I managed!"

What have I gotten myself into this time?

"The new shirt, the combed hair. Not speaking out of turn. Saying nothing unexpected. Just being so normal! Dreadfully, drearily, predictably normal! An excellent challenge, Maria. But you must agree I passed."

"I guess so," I muttered.

"Yes!" he exclaimed. I thought I heard him do a fist pump. "And now I present your first challenge, Maria."

"You don't say."

"Oh, I do. And, taking a cue from you, it involves doing the unexpected. Straying from your customary role. Upsetting the applecart of convention. To zig where others—"

"You already said that one."

"Zag. To zig where others zag."

If I wanted him off the porch by the time the bus came, my best chance was to play along. "What's the challenge?" I asked.

"Your challenge, dear Maria, seems simple at first. Deceptively simple. But I believe you will find it a challenge enough."

"Okay, okay. What is it?"

"Today, you shall use a certain word in math class."

I bit: "What word?"

"Rutabaga," he cried triumphantly.

"*Rutabaga?*" I asked.

"The Swedish turnip," he replied. "A root vegetable, common across Europe, which—"

"I know what a rutabaga is," I told him. "I just don't know why you want me to say it. Why on earth would I say *rutabaga?*"

"Precisely!" he yelled. "There is no reason! That's just the point! I want you to say it because it is not something you would normally do. I want you to say it *because it is not something you want to do.* You need only say it once to pass the challenge. It will take mere seconds. Simple, as I said. Painless. But a challenge nonetheless."

"I can't believe you," I said.

"Then you should try a little harder," JJ said with a smile in his voice. "I'm not so hard to believe."

Before I could think of what to say to *that*, JJ's mom called from down the block. "JJ, come home, it's time to go!" JJ rode to school with his mom and sister. They dropped Cynthia off at a special school somewhere, where there was a whole class of kids like her. Then his mom took him to Marble City Middle. They had offered—more than once— for me to ride with them. It was quicker than the bus, but I turned them down. For obvious reasons. And I'd never been happier with that decision than right now.

"Gotta go," JJ said. "But I'll see you in math class!"

"See ya."

"Rutabaga!" he cried and shuffled down the sidewalk.

Fat chance, JJ, I thought. JJ can be crazy if he wants. Everyone expects him to be weird, and besides, he can get away with it. Not me. I'm weird enough already, with my glass eyeballs and my long cane and my bumpy books. No point in adding to the list. Like I said, I don't like to call attention to myself.

When others zag?

I think I'll zag too.

10

Things You Might Be Wondering, Part Three: Roxie

The third question I get a lot is about my cane. Roxanne. (Or Roxie, for short. What can I say? *Esmerelda* was too pretty. *Luella* was too country. And *Susie* just felt wrong.) I carry her everywhere I go. My cane teacher, Mr. Torres, tells me my cane is a forty-two-inch aluminum folding mobility cane, red and white, with a straight grip and a roller hook tip. But I just call her Roxie.

Mr. Torres says Roxie makes my arms longer, so I can feel things far away, things I can't see. Like potholes, or flagpoles, or the stupid backpack that Tommy left in the middle of the freakin' hallway. Roxie also helps me find the top of the staircase at school. (It's always good to know where the top of the staircase is.)

Plus she helps me hear things. The *tap-tap-tap* of a blind kid using a cane? That's not just noise to me. It's news. Each tap sounds different, depending where I am. Hallways sound different than rooms, concrete sounds different than metal. I can tell where a doorway is just by the way the sound bounces back to me, if I'm paying attention. Roxie helps with that.

I take lessons once a week with Mr. Torres. When I was young, he taught me how to use the cane, sweeping it back and forth in front of me, tapping when I needed to, probing out and around me. Finding fire hydrants before I ran into them. That sort of thing. Now all that stuff is second nature, and we spend our time finding new places and exploring them, trying to learn our way around.

"Use your cane and your brain," he says, "and figure it out."

Sometimes I do and sometimes I don't. But most of the time, I do.

11

Where and How

Mr. Torres comes every Wednesday at ten a.m. for my O&M lesson. O&M stands for Orientation & Mobility, which is just a fancy name for my cane class. It's when we leave school and head into town to explore. I use my cane and my brain, like I already told you, but I also use the sounds and smells and all sorts of tiny little clues that tell me where I am. It helps to prepare me for when I'll be older and on my own, finding my way around towns and cities and stores and airports by myself.

I think the words *orientation* and *mobility* are confusing and Mr. Torres agrees. He told me that *orientation* is knowing where you are, and *mobility* is knowing how to get where you want to go. And that is what he teaches: *where* and *how*. He says they just use those fancy words to make it sound scientific, so he can get paid more. I think he's joking but I'm not sure.

He also says that, if I want to, instead of calling it *Orientation & Mobility*, we can call it *Where & How* class.

Mr. Torres says that's a better name anyway, because most of our work can be boiled down into three questions:

Do You Know Where You Are?
Do You Know Where You're Going?
Do You Know How to Get There?

He calls those the Three Golden Questions of cane class, and he asks them all the time.

And if I can't answer one?

Mr. Torres won't tell me.

Use your cane and your brain, he'll say, for the hundredth time. *And figure it out.*

I've been working with Mr. Torres once a week since I was five years old, so we've gotten kind of tight. He's like an uncle to me. When we head out to do lessons, we usually have five or ten minutes in his car, on our way to whatever neighborhood, strip mall, or stoplight he wants me to figure out that day.

That's when Mr. Torres likes to talk to me about how traffic works. I know that sounds like Dullsville to you, but it's kinda important for a kid like me. Remember, I don't see this stuff. So Mr. Torres tells me about it. He tells me what the cars are doing and how the roads run together, and how there are all these signs and lights and lines on the road that tell people what to do. The *rules of the road*, he calls them. He says I need to understand them, even if I'll never ever drive, or at least not until our cars are total robots and do all our driving for us, which might be in ten years, or might be in a hundred.

Sometimes, on rainy days, we don't go out at all, but just sit in the library with little toy cars. Mr. Torres will use felt and buttons and strips of Velcro to create different intersections: a four-way stop sign, a residential cul-de-sac, a six-lane divided highway with turn lanes on either side. He'll lay them out for me, gives me a brief introduction, and then it's my job to move the cars around according to the *rules of the road*.

The one on your right, the pickup truck. What lane can he turn into? Mr. Torres will ask.

The southbound lane just got a green light, he'll say. *Show me how the cars will move now.*

What's a right turn on red? Who can take one?

It's harder than you might think, if you've never seen traffic. I'm forever moving cars into the wrong lane, turning them left when I mean to turn them right, wheeling them across two lanes of traffic in the middle of an intersection.

Mr. Torres chuckles when I do this, and gently corrects me, but I don't think it's funny. I'm worried that if I don't figure all this stuff out, the first time they turn me loose in town there's gonna be a Maria Pancake on the streets of Marble City.

That won't happen, Mr. Torres says.

But I'm not so sure.

Right now it's just talk, because I haven't been turned loose yet. I'm not allowed out on my own, not by myself. Oh sure, I can walk down my block, maybe visit the houses closest to me. I can go to JJ's if I want to. (Not that I want to.) But Mr. Torres says it's not a good idea for me to be crossing streets by myself yet. There's still too much to learn.

So, yes, it's true: even though I'm a sixth grader, I don't walk alone. I've never walked by myself to the bakery that's four blocks from my house, never crossed a street by myself. Mr. Torres says it's coming, I'm closer than I think. He also says we'll practice it a hundred times, or maybe a thousand, before I do it on my own, but I'll be honest: it scares the daylights out of me.

Mr. Torres says not to worry. Mr. Torres says I'm smarter than I think. Mr. Torres says we'll leave the pancakes for the breakfast plate.

I wish I could believe him.

12

Gumshoe

So that's Roxie, and me, and canes and brains and Where and How. And since it was Wednesday today, Mr. Torres came at ten o'clock, just like he does every week. He took me out to a neighborhood I'd never been to, and had me figure out what the traffic was doing, when it was moving and when it was about to move, and when would be a safe time to cross the street.

When we do this, I mostly just listen and wait. I stand there. And listen. And wait. Then I listen and wait some more, and try not to let my mind wander, because this is serious business you know, and then after some more listening and waiting I decide it's time to trust in myself and step into the street.

And then, one of two things happens.

If I'm right, and it's safe to cross, Mr. Torres does nothing. He lets me cross the street and find the other side.

But if I'm wrong, I feel his hand on my shoulder, stopping me from stepping into the oncoming traffic.

Today, I tried to cross the street twenty times. Sixteen times I did it right. The other four times he stopped me.

Pretty good, right?

Wrong.

That was four times I might've gotten killed, four Maria Pancakes on the streets of Marble City.

And that's not good enough.

But Mr. Torres must have been satisfied, because on our way back to school, instead of lecturing me about T-shaped intersections, Mr. Torres asked me what was on my mind.

We do that sometimes. Mr. Torres says that every single conversation doesn't have to be about traffic. Mr. Torres says that, as much as he loves traffic, even he can't talk about it all day long. So instead we'll just talk about what's up in my life. Life outside the crosswalk, he calls it.

"How's life outside the crosswalk?" he asked me today.

"Better than life inside the crosswalk," I told him.

"Take it easy on yourself," Mr. Torres said. "It's coming."

"Doesn't feel like it," I said.

"Does to me," he said. "But enough of that. Tell me, Maria. How's life outside the crosswalk?"

So, I decided to tell him about JJ and the challenges and his superhero detective agency nonsense. I gave him the whole story, including a few choice words about JJ.

"The Twinnoggin Detective Agency?" Mr. Torres asked when I was done. "What do you think?"

"I just told you. I think it's nonsense."

Mr. Torres laughed.

"What?" I said.

"Nothing," he said.

"It's never nothing, Mr. Torres."

"I was just thinking how you're already a pretty good detective."

"Come again?"

"Face it, Maria," he said. "You *are* a detective. You show it to me every day. Take this morning's lesson. We went to a new neighborhood, somewhere you'd never been. We drove all across town to get there, a dozen turns or more, and I pulled up next to a sidewalk you'd never ever stood on and will never ever see. You got out of the car and told me, right away, that you were facing south. How did you know?"

"The sun," I say. We've talked about this before. "In the morning the sun is in the east, so if it's on my left cheek, I know I'm facing south."

"Bingo," Mr. Torres said. "A little while later you were

crossing a new street. Montgomery Avenue. You'd already figured out it was four lanes, maybe five with a turn lane, based on the traffic you'd heard, but you'd never actually walked across it. There was no way to know just how wide the street was. Could be forty feet, could be sixty-five. And yet, as you approached the far curb, a few steps from the edge, I saw you lift your cane tip slightly, anticipating the sidewalk. How did you know it was there?"

"The slope of the road. Most of the streets in Marble City slope to let the rainwater run off. I knew I had passed the crown of the street, which I took to be somewhere near the center. But right next to the gutter the slope got steeper. That meant I was almost to the sidewalk. Time to feel for the curb."

"Elementary, my dear Romero," Mr. Torres said. "Three weeks ago. It's raining, so we're working the big grocery store on Kingston Pike. That place is like a maze, and I'm doing my best to get you lost inside of it. We've made about twenty turns—there's no way you can remember them all. And yet as soon as I say it's time to go, you head straight for the front doors. How did you know where they were?"

"That one's easy, Mr. T. I listened for the checkout lines. The beep of the scanners. They're almost always by the front door, but I knew for sure because I heard them when I first came in the store."

"You see?" Mr. Torres said. "You already are a detective, Maria. You know left from right, two o'clock from ten o'clock, northwest from southeast. You know what it sounds like when your cane tip hits a sewer grate, a bus stop, or a patch of ice. You can tell a stop sign from a stoplight just by listening to the cars. You can tell the height of the ceiling the minute you walk into a room. You notice things."

"Some things, anyway."

"Lots of things," Mr. Torres said. "As far as I'm concerned, you're a regular gumshoe. So go ahead and tell JJ that you've

already graduated. Tell him you're already a first-rate, bona
fide, blue-ribbon clue collector. Not only that, you know
what those clues mean. You figure out what's around you,
what just happened, and what might happen next. So, what
was once a mystery is now as plain as day. That's all there is to
Orientation & Mobility, Maria. How and Where, and a little
bit of Why. Piece of cake."

"But not pancake," I say.

"Never pancake," he says.

Just then, I felt Mr. Torres' car slow and take a hard right,
followed by a short uphill and a curve to the left: we were
getting close to school.

"Thanks, Mr. T.," I said, "for your vote of confidence."

"No problem."

"I'll tell JJ you said I can forget all his craziness. I'm already
a detective."

"That's right," he said.

"A real pro."

"The best."

"And I don't need to mess with JJ and his crazy rutabaga,"
I said. "You said so."

"Rutabaga?" Mr. Torres asked.

I told him about JJ's dumb-as-a-rock challenge, about me
saying the word *rutabaga* in math class. I told him not only
was it as dumb as a rock, but it was as dumb as a dumb rock.
And that's pretty dumb.

"*Rutabaga?*" he cried when I was done.

"Yes," I hissed.

"The Swedish turnip?"

"Yes."

"In math class?"

"*Yes.*"

"Ha!" Mr. Torres laughed. He drummed his fingers on
the steering wheel. "I think you should do it, Maria."

"What? What are you, crazy?"

"Perhaps. But why not?"

"It's weird is why not," I said. "Nobody says the word *rutabaga* in math class."

"Precisely."

"That's his whole point, of course. He wants me to zig where others zag. Get outside of my comfort zone."

"Hmmm."

"But I don't see the benefit. You know why they call it a comfort zone, right, Mr. Torres?"

"Why?"

"Because it's comfortable there," I said.

Mr. Torres didn't say anything.

"There's nothing wrong with a little comfort," I added.

Still he didn't say anything.

"I mean, if there was a good reason to do it, then maybe. If I was going to win a trophy or help out a friend or save a baby puppy or something. But there's no rhyme or reason to this. It makes no sense."

"Not much," Mr. Torres admitted.

"I'm not too scared to do it," I said. "Just too smart."

"Fair enough," said Mr. Torres.

"I mean, JJ's crazy, right? Total nutjob."

"Your words, not mine. I'd never say that about a kid."

"Well, you don't know JJ."

"I don't," Mr. Torres acknowledged. "Still, if I were you, I'd be careful, Maria."

"Be careful of what?"

"Don't be so quick to judge another."

"There's nothing quick about it," I said. "JJ's been weird since the day I met him."

"I bet I'd like him. He sounds like an interesting kid."

"Interesting? That's one word for it."

We were parked now. Cane class was over. All that was left was for me to hop out of the car and head back to the school building. But I could tell Mr. Torres wasn't done. I heard him shift his weight and pull his keys from the ignition. He didn't say goodbye.

"I think you should do it," he announced.

"What?"

"Do it. Say *rutabaga* in math class."

"Why?"

"Never pass up a chance to be different, especially when you're young. The world needs more weird."

"That sounds like something JJ would say."

"Perhaps."

"The way I see it, my job is to be as *normal* as I can be."

"Perhaps."

"*My* world needs more *normal*, Mr. Torres. Not more weird. I've got weird down."

"Maybe so," he said.

I got out of the car, listened for the flags flapping in front of the main entrance, and turned in that direction. As I was pulling my backpack over my shoulders and closing the car door, Mr. Torres added a final thought:

"And maybe not."

13

Zig

I still can't explain it.

An hour later I was sitting in math class, half-daydreaming and half-listening as Ms. Griffin went over the answers to last night's homework.

When she got to Number 12 and asked who could tell her the greatest common factor of 34 and 51, I raised my hand. Ms. Griffin called on me. "Maria?"

What I said next surprised even me.

"Rutabaga."

I said it loud and clear and confident. Makayla and Jasmine snickered behind me.

"Excuse me?" Ms. Griffin said.

"Seventeen," I said. "Seventeen is the greatest common factor of thirty-four and fifty-one."

"That's correct. Thank you, Maria."

"That was random," Makayla said. But of course it wasn't. It was exactly what JJ had asked me to do. I had completed my first challenge.

Why had I done it? I couldn't tell you then and I can't tell you now. I wasn't planning on it.

Maybe I just wanted to prove I could do it. Maybe I was tired of always doing and saying the right thing. Maybe JJ was right: it was time for me to zig where others zagged, if only in this tiny little way. Maybe Mr. Torres was right: the world needs more weird.

It wasn't much, really. I just said one word. I just said *rutabaga* instead of *seventeen*. I'm not sure Mrs. Griffin even noticed or thought much about it at any rate. It was silly, a dare. A tiny little act of rebellion in a life lived by the book. It was stupid.

So why did it feel so good?

14

Not the Blind Girl

It didn't feel so good by fourth period. Because that's about how long it took for me to get my new nickname at Marble City Middle.

Rutabaga Girl.

It started with Hannah, then Kaitlyn, then Jasmine, and by the end of the day, half of the school was calling me Rutabaga Girl.

"What's up, Rutabaga?" Evie said when I passed her on my way to English.

"Rutabaga Girl comin' through!" Annabelle shouted when I made my way up to the front of Mrs. Kent's room to turn in my vocabulary homework.

"Have a good day, Baga Baby!" Kaitlyn trilled when she saw me getting on the bus, which caused what sounded like about a hundred people to break out laughing.

I stewed all the way home, embarrassed and ashamed and angry. Angry at JJ, sure, for giving me the challenge, and angry at Mr. Torres for letting me think somehow, even just for a minute, that it was a good idea. But more than that I was angry with myself. Whatever little piece of *normal* I could lay claim to I'd gotten by being smart and careful and precise. Mama's little scientist. And now I'd thrown it all away on some half-hearted meaningless joke. I'd given up on cold plain logic for the promise of a stupid dream. The dream that it was okay for me to be different, if only for a minute. To zig where others zag.

So much for that idea.

So you can imagine how annoyed I was to find JJ on my

porch when I got home. He was the last person on earth I wanted to see.

"Congratulations!" JJ cried as soon as I hit the first step. "You did it! You passed the first challenge!"

"Whoopty-doo," I said.

"I must admit, I didn't think you would do it. But you did! I'm so proud of you!"

"That makes one of us."

"Aw, come on, Maria. It was beautiful!"

"That's not the word I would choose."

JJ paused. I made a dark and angry face, eyebrows down.

"What's bothering you?" he asked.

"What's bothering me?" I cried. "What's bothering me? How about the whole school laughing at me? How about that? How's that for bothersome? Not good enough? How about my new nickname being Rutabaga Girl? How about that!"

"Who called you Rutabaga Girl?"

"Just everybody," I said. "Just Hannah, just Kaitlyn, just everybody!"

"Good," JJ said.

"*Good?*" I cried. "Did you say, *Good?*"

"Good," he repeated.

"And how, JJ? How on earth is everyone at school calling me *Rutabaga Girl,* and *Baga Baby,* and *Queen Rutabaga*…how is that *good?*"

"Simple," JJ said. "You're not the blind girl anymore."

"What?"

"Oh, you're still a blind girl," JJ said, "but you're not *The Blind Girl.* See what I mean?"

"No."

"You've been complaining for years that, whenever anybody sees you, all they can see is *The Blind Girl.* Well, here's your chance. Your chance to be defined by something other than whether you can see."

"Humph."

"I mean, blind is fine and all. Blind is great. You do a great job of being blind. But isn't it better to be known by something you *did*, rather than just by something you *are*?"

"I guess that depends on what you *did*," I said. "If what you *did* makes you feel weird, and dumb, and different, then maybe not."

"Fair enough," said JJ. "But that part's up to you."

"What part?"

"Feeling weird and dumb and different. I could say *rutabaga* in class and not feel weird or dumb or different. So the part where you feel weird and dumb and different? That part's up to you."

"Whatever."

"It's true."

"I don't see what my feelings have to do with it. It's not about what I feel. If I say *rutabaga* in math class, people are going to think I'm weird and dumb and different, no matter how I feel about it."

"Like who?"

"Like everyone. Hannah, Kaitlyn, Makayla, all of them."

"So?"

"So I don't want them thinking that about me. Unlike you, I care what other people think of me. That's not a crime, you know. To care what other people think of you."

"No," he said. "It's not a crime."

"I'm weird and different enough already. I don't need to add dumb."

"You make a good point," JJ said. "It's not good to feel dumb. But weird and different? Weird and different has its place."

"Easy for you to say."

"Not really," said JJ. "It took me a long time to get there. But I'm glad I did."

"Good for you," I said.

"Yep," he agreed. "Good for me."

If having JJ on my porch when I got home from school wasn't annoying enough, having him on my porch lecturing me about how great it was to be weird and different definitely was. I was pretty fed up by the time I heard JJ's mom calling him from down the block. It must have been his turn to watch Cynthia.

"Sorry, I've got to go," JJ said. "But I feel like we're getting somewhere. I'll be back tomorrow, and we can pick up where we left off."

"I don't think so, JJ," I said. "Please don't come."

"Why is that?"

"Because I'm tired of it, JJ. I'm tired of it all. I'm tired of the detective agency, I'm tired of the challenges, and I am most definitely tired of the rutabagas. It's all nonsense. Stupid little third grade nonsense. I'm trying to grow up here, JJ."

"Aren't we all?"

"And I don't think this is helping. Listen, JJ. I tried your stupid challenge. I said *rutabaga*, and all it got me was laughed out of math class. I'm done, JJ. I don't want to play your game anymore."

"Maria, I—"

"No, JJ. Drop it. Just drop it."

"But I want—"

"You're standing on my porch, JJ. So this is not about what you want. It's about what I want. And what I want is for you to leave me alone."

There was silence for a while. It was probably only a few seconds, but it felt longer. Part of me was worried that I had hurt him. Part of me didn't care. I could hear him breathing, in and out, and I knew he hadn't moved.

I waited.

"I'm raising my eyebrows and looking at you quizzically," JJ finally announced. His voice was quieter now, more subdued.

"Thank you for that information."

"And now my features are falling, and I'm looking a little disappointed."

"Good."

"And now I have the *Oh Well* look on my face. A look that says, *When someone asks you to leave their porch, you should leave their porch.*"

"And now let's talk about my face," I said. "You know I'm not too good with expressions, but if I'm doing it right, I hope my face says, *Go on, then. Just leave me alone.*" I lowered my eyelids and took all expression from my lips.

JJ said, "Yep. That's what your face says."

"I guess I'll get going, then," he added. "So long, Maria."

The mustard smell left first, then the wet wheeze, and finally the heavy boots plodding down my sidewalk, away, away, away. I breathed a sigh of relief.

So long, JJ.

15

Left Alone

You've probably already guessed what happened next.

Yep.

That knothead took my last words—*Leave Me Alone*—as his second challenge.

He did it too. He left me alone for a whole week. Not a word about the detective agency. Not a word about our honor. Not a word about rutabagas. Not even a hello in the hallway. It was nice, nice and quiet, but it couldn't last. Because by leaving me alone, JJ was just digging in deeper. By leaving me alone, he was playing the game. Doubling down. I had given him a challenge, and he had accepted it.

Game over?

Not a chance.

Game on.

In other news, my new nickname stuck to me like glue. Everyone in school, from the sixth grade to the eighth, knew me as *Rutabaga Girl*. Whatever glimmer of hope I had that Hannah and Kaitlyn would take me into their circle had faded to almost nothing. Sure, they were still nice to me in front of the teacher—you can't be caught picking on a blind girl, after all, not in this enlightened age—but when the teachers weren't around, I was *Rutabaga Girl. Little Miss Rutabaga. Baga Baby.*

"You don't need those girls anyway," my mom said when we talked about it over dinner. "If that's the way they act, they're no friends of yours."

"They're no friends of mine. You got that part right, Mom. That much is true."

"And they don't need to be," my mom said.

But she forgets. She forgets what it is like to be in the sixth grade. Maybe Hannah and Kaitlyn and Jasmine don't need to be my friends. But someone does. Someone other than Chloe. Someone other than Sam, who is a thousand miles away. Someone other than JJ. Someone other than Mom. Is that too much to ask?

So I was feeling kind of blue and burned and stupid and alone, which is not a great way to feel, not for anybody. Mom says there's a place for all kinds of feelings in a person's life, even blue and burned and stupid and alone. She says that she's felt that way, too, plenty of times, and it's no fun but it's part of what makes us human. The point is not to get stuck there, she says. Notice those feelings when they come by, she says, maybe even spend a day or two with them, but don't invite them to move into your house.

That seems like good advice, and I was trying to take it, but I was worried that the feelings meant to move in anyway, whether I invited them or not. It didn't seem like they were going to go away anytime soon, that's for sure.

I didn't see JJ for a whole week, not until the next Wednesday afternoon, exactly one week after the whole *rutabaga* business got started. I was at home sick, or at least pretending to be sick, when Mom got a call from JJ's mom, Mary Munson. Mary told my mom that she was held up at a doctor's appointment, and asked if we could pick up Cynthia when her school let out at 2:30. Mom said sure, we'd be happy to help. She told me to get my shoes on, we were heading out. I tried to tell her I didn't need to go with her, I could stay home alone, but she wasn't having any of it.

"Not with you on your deathbed," she added. I couldn't see but it sure sounded like she was winking when she said this. "I wouldn't dream of leaving you alone right now."

The next thing I knew I was in the car on the way to Kenesaw Elementary, which is the school on the west side of town that has the special program for kids with autism. We parked and went inside.

I had never been to Kenesaw before, so instead of tapping my way down the unfamiliar hallways towards Cynthia's room, I picked up my cane and let Mom be my sighted guide. If you haven't heard of *sighted guide* before, it's when I take the elbow of someone with good eyeballs, and let them be my guide. My sighted guide.

I mean, I'm a detective, right? Mr. Torres had told me as much. But let me tell you something about being a detective: it's exhausting. Sure, there are days when I'm up for it. Days when I want something new and challenging, days when I want to use my cane and my brain, just like Mr. Torres says. But there are also days—plenty of them—where the last thing I want to do is to go some place I've never been before, and have to figure out the halls, walls, windows, and doors from scratch. (To say nothing of the curbs, stairs, and signposts trying to put a knot in my head.) So as often as not, when we're somewhere new, like say a restaurant or Mom's employee picnic or Kenesaw Elementary, I'll grab my mom's elbow and let her lead me.

I still pay attention, even when I'm on her elbow. I'll pay attention to distance, notice turns, listen for an open doorway—so I can get a sense of the place. I count stairs when we go up or down them, so on the way back I know what to expect. It's still work, but it's not nearly as much work as it is when I have to figure it all out by myself.

Oh, and here's a blind-person tip if you ever need one: when you meet a blind person, and you're trying to help them find something, don't just grab onto them and start dragging. Every once in a while, some well-meaning soul will just grab my wrist and start dragging me along, like I'm a wagon that needs to be pulled to a mulch pile. Other times, someone might latch onto my shoulders and push me through space, like I'm a wheelbarrow and he's a happy farmer finishing up his morning chores. But I'd rather not be a wagon or a wheelbarrow—I do better as a sidecar. Let me hold on to your elbow, and walk about a half-step behind you. You can do all the seeing, steering, and stopping, and I'll hang on for the ride. Easy-peasy.

I took Mom's elbow and we went down to Cynthia's classroom to pick her up. It wasn't a big deal: Mom was on the list of people who could pick Cynthia up, and she had done it a few times before, but this was the first time I was along for the ride. She talked briefly to Cynthia's teacher, and then it was time to go.

And then Cynthia grabbed *my* elbow.

She had seen how I was holding on to Mom, and I guess it gave her an idea. She just reached out and grabbed on to me. Now, Cynthia can see everything around her, and she walks just fine by herself, so it's not like she needed any help. I guess she just wanted to hold on to me the way I held on to Mom.

I didn't mind—it felt kind of nice, actually—but I didn't expect we would walk that way. But then Mom said, *Let's Go*, and started walking. Of course I held on and followed her, and Cynthia held on to me and followed both of us, and so there we were, a three-person chain moving through the halls of Kenesaw Elementary. We must have looked absurd, because Mom started laughing, and then Cynthia started laughing with her, and in spite of myself I started laughing, too, and then there we were, the three of us together, walking and laughing and carrying on all the way out to the car, like we didn't have a care in the world. I felt better than I had all week.

On the drive home Mom was in a goofy mood and she was getting me and Cynthia there too. Cynthia doesn't speak, remember, but she has her ways of letting us know what she's feeling. She giggled from time to time and made sounds that, while they weren't words, or at least not words that you or I would recognize, they were definitely sounds of joy and contentment. It was a nice ride.

Of course, it also meant I'd have to see JJ again. I couldn't see a way around it. Once he got home from Marble City Middle, he'd be coming over to pick up Cynthia, and Mom would expect me to say hello, to greet him on the porch and, worse, *be nice* to him. So while my mood had improved significantly, and while it was nice to hang out with Cynthia— Mom gave us milk and gingersnaps when we got home—the whole time I was trying to dream up a way to get out of seeing JJ, to get out of hearing him share his latest thoughts about the Twinnoggin Superhero Detective Challenge.

I guess I'm not that smart, because I didn't come up with a plan by the time JJ arrived. Sure enough, Mom pushed me out on the porch to say hello and chat with him while she gathered Cynthia's things.

"And so, my dear Maria, we meet again," JJ said as I shuffled onto the porch.

"I see you brought my sister," he added, and indeed I had. Cynthia had clutched on to my elbow again, I'm not sure why. I think she thought it was funny.

"Yep," I said. "We've had a good time." Truth is, I found her better company than I found him, but I didn't say so, not with Mom standing nearby.

"I see she still has a cookie," JJ said. She must have been holding the gingersnap Mom had given her.

"Very observant," I said.

"She does love her sweets."

"I see."

"I have completed my second challenge, Maria."

Sigh.

"I have left you alone for a week now. Surely that is long enough to prove my merit. I must say, Maria, I'd hoped your challenges for me would be more imaginative than *be normal* and *leave you alone*. That's what everyone else wants me to do, after all: be normal and leave them alone. I was looking forward to something a little more mysterious."

I held my tongue.

"But that is your choice, and not mine," he blathered on. "I have been faithful to your word. I trust my efforts have not gone unnoticed."

"No, JJ, they haven't."

"And so the coin flips once again, and it is my turn to challenge you once more."

This kid is unreal, I thought. "JJ—"

"But not today," he interrupted. "Your first challenge required both forethought and intent. You had a decision to make, a decision that required a change of perspective, and a moment of bravery besides. As I have noted before, you passed with flying colors. Your next challenge shall be more—how shall I say it?—*impromptu* in nature. There will not be so much time to think, only to react. It is a test of another kind."

"Great," I said, not meaning it. "Sounds delightful," I added, not meaning that either.

"Oh, I don't know about *delightful*," JJ said. "Delightful is not the point. But already I have said too much." He clopped down the stairs and out to the street, with Cynthia following after.

"Fare thee well, Maria," he called out. "Be on your toes."

Oh, cripes, I thought. His footfalls hadn't even left the driveway yet, and I was already worried about what he would pull next. There was no use in trying to get out of it. He'd find me. He always found me.

When you can't see someone coming, it's awfully hard to hide.

16

My Crabby-Abby Days Top Ten List of the Most

Annoying Things About Being Blind,

In No Particular Order,

Numbers 4-7

4. I'm not deaf. I hear just fine. You don't have to yell at me.

5. People who get all quiet when I come around, like they're scared of me

6. Getting more help than I need

7. Getting less help than I need

17

Antonio

Say this about JJ: he's true to his word. When we got back to school on Thursday, he didn't even wait until lunchtime to pull his next stunt. It was right after first period. I was standing at my locker, talking to Chloe and fishing in my backpack for my math folder. (I have braille labels on all of them, so I can tell what's what without even pulling them from my backpack.) My fingers had just found *Math* when JJ came shuffling up. The hallway was crowded—Kaitlyn and Hannah were right next to us, and Jasmine and Makayla were about three lockers down—but when JJ shuffles up, people make way for him. I've never straight up measured it, but my guess is that most students at Marble City Middle do their level best to keep a two-foot buffer between their bodies and JJ's at any given time. Let's just say he never lacks for elbow room.

I could tell it was JJ even before he opened his mouth; above the murmur of the hall I heard his wheeze and shuffle.

I stood there fiddling with my push-button lock, doing my best to ignore my un-ignore-able neighbor.

"Good morning, Maria!" JJ exclaimed, about twice as loud as needed. He must have wanted to make sure the whole hall was watching.

"Good morning, JJ," I mumbled.

"Are you ready for your next challenge?"

"Challenge?" Hannah asked.

Oh man. Not Hannah. The cat wasn't quite out of the bag, not just yet, about me and JJ and the detective agency and his stupid challenges. But you could see a paw sticking out.

"Yes, Hannah, *challenge*. Defined in the dictionary as 'A call to take part in a contest or competition, as in a duel.' C-h-a-l-l-e-n-g-e. Challenge."

"I know that, dimwit," Hannah spat.

"Dimwit?" JJ repeated. "*Dimwit?* Hannah, I thought you could do better. I have many faults, it's true. I'm odd at times. A strange duck. My hair's a mess, my clothes don't match, and I'm a touch overweight."

"A touch?"

"But whatever else I am, I am not dim-witted. I'm sure in your vast experience of putting people down—of making people feel small so that you could feel big—you could have chosen a more appropriate insult."

I cringed.

"I'll do better next time," Hannah assured him.

"I look forward to it," JJ said. "Now, where was I? Ah yes, your challenge."

"Challenge?" Hannah asked again. She was goading him now. She couldn't afford to back down from the likes of JJ Munson.

I braced myself for JJ's next rambling gassy barb, but he said nothing. Instead, he unzipped his backpack and placed something long and spongy in my hands.

I felt it, slowly, working to figure out what on earth it was. I was a little annoyed—*Can You Guess What This Thing Is?* is nearly as bad a blind-person carnival game as *Can You Guess Whose Voice This Is?*—but what else could I do? It felt like the whole hall was watching. I scanned it with my hands. It had bumps all over it, and felt a little clammy. It had a body, two legs, a long neck, and a head. And was that a beak on one end?

"Is that a rubber chicken?" Hannah exclaimed.

JJ Munson had just placed a rubber chicken in my hands,

right in front of God, Hannah, and everybody, and now I was stuck holding the thing.

"Indeed, it is a rubber chicken," JJ confirmed. "But not just any rubber chicken. This one is named Antonio."

"Antonio," Hannah said. "How sweet."

"Your challenge, Maria, is to have Antonio on Mr. Zukowski's desk in the next twenty-four hours."

"What?" I cried.

"It will require stealth and cunning, that is true. Nimble feet, to be sure, and a nimble mind as well. But I am sure you are up to the task."

"He'll kill me," I said.

"Pfft," JJ dismissed me. "Reports of his murderous past are greatly exaggerated. I have vast experience in this regard. You may wish you were dead, but he won't actually kill you."

"That's comforting," I said.

"We'll report back here at this time tomorrow, Doña Romero. I look forward to hearing of your success."

"Okay," I muttered.

"Or failure," JJ added, and with that he shuffled off to his locker, no doubt to do some weird JJ-type thing, like see how many paperclips he could fit in each nostril.

"What the—?" Hannah asked.

"Never mind," I said, stuffing Antonio as deep into my backpack as I could make him go.

"That was random," she said.

"He's got a few screws loose," I said.

"More than a few. Why do you let him talk to you?"

"I don't have much choice. He finds me. Besides, he's my neighbor. Mom says I've got to be nice to him."

"That's why you shouldn't do everything your mom says," Hannah snorted.

Just then, JJ came bumbling back by on his return trip from his locker. "See you tomorrow, Romero!" he chirped.

"Go sit on a pole, JJ," I spat.

Which, when you come to think about it, is exactly what I *shouldn't* have said.

❧

You've probably figured out already that JJ was going to take my words literally, and go and find himself a pole to sit on. The only questions that remained: What kind of pole? And where?

Let us consider the options.

Would he find a simple fence pole, like the sort that holds up chain-link fencing? There were plenty of those around, including dozens right out in the school parking lot.

Nahhh. Too easy.

Would he set his sights a little higher, and settle down on that big pole out on the blacktop that holds up the basketball hoop? That thing was ten feet off the ground, but nothing JJ couldn't tackle with a ladder and a few big wheezy mustard grunts to hoist himself up. I could almost picture him up atop the backboard, hollering my name and probably writing poems to the pigeons while he was up there.

Perhaps.

Or maybe he'd go whimsical this time and find himself a barbershop pole. That one I could definitely picture: he'd bring it into math class, plug it in so it lit up and spun, and spend a lesson on obtuse angles perched atop that candy-striped column. Ms. Griffin would probably let him too. She has a soft spot for weirdos. (Lots of adults do, I've noticed, but not many kids. I wonder why.)

Whatever he was going to do, I wasn't biting. Challenge refused. Antonio the Rubber Chicken was stuffed deep down in my backpack, and that's where he was going to stay, at least until I decided whether to give him back to JJ—at home, of course, as far away from school as possible—or just toss him in the nearest trash can. One thing I was *not* going to do was put him on Mr. Zukowski's desk.

18

Quite a Morning

I didn't have to wait a long time to see what JJ cooked up. Unless you consider one day a long time.

It was Friday morning, eight o'clock. I was on the school bus, and we had just turned into the driveway in front of Marble City Middle. I had been chatting with Chloe and fiddling with my phone when I heard a buzz and titter up and down the aisles of the bus. Through the open windows I could hear a large crowd gathered outside.

The buzz on the bus grew louder, and then a kid named Mitchell cried out, "What's going on?"

"Up there," someone else chimed in. (I think it was Anaya, but I couldn't be sure.)

"What's he doing?" another kid hollered, and in moments those isolated shouts turned into the steady din of thirty kids screaming their lungs out on Bus 107.

"Look at him!"

"Think it will hold him?"

"Who the heck is that?"

The crowd outside grew louder too, and as the bus idled at the curb I heard the buzz of Mr. Zukowski's voice over a megaphone. "Calm down, everyone. Calm down! I need everyone to report to homeroom!"

Nobody moved, as far as I could tell. The clamor just grew louder.

"Everyone to homeroom!" Zukowski hollered again.

"What's going on?" I whispered to Chloe as we made our way down the aisle of the bus.

"It's JJ," she said.

Of course it is, I thought. "What about him?"

Chloe answered slowly, one phrase at a time, as if she could scarcely believe what she was seeing. "He's up. On top. Of the flagpole."

"The flagpole?"

"Yeah, the flagpole. He's tied himself in somehow. He's got all this gear on, like a mountain climber. He's way up there."

"How high?" I asked.

"I don't know. Twenty-five feet? Forty? Higher than the roof, that's for sure."

We stepped off the bus. Kids were milling about, moving in all directions, without a rhyme or reason as far as I could tell. It was a madhouse.

Madhouse crowds are not ideal for kids who walk with a cane. It's one of the few times people don't notice you coming. It's easy to get stuck, easy to feel like you're about to get trampled. My friend Sam has a trick he uses in these situations: he just lets that cane loose, slinging it from side to side, and starts hollering, "Blind kid coming through!" Works like a charm, he says. Like Moses parting the waters.

I didn't have that kind of moxie, but I did find myself swinging Roxie in wider and wider arcs, wider for sure than Mr. Torres had taught me, just to make sure all those distracted kids knew I was there. I might have hit a few ankles, but at least I had a little space to move.

"Everyone to homeroom!" Mr. Zukowski ordered again over the megaphone, before turning his attention to JJ. "Young man, I need you to stay right where you are, and hold onto that pole. We have the fire department on their way."

"I don't need the fire department," JJ called down. "I know what I'm doing. I've got my gear. I'm perfectly safe."

I wondered how long he'd been up there, and how he got there in the first place.

Despite Mr. Zukowski's pleas, the crowd was not getting any thinner. If anything, it was getting thicker. I made it to the front door and turned to listen to the noise. It seemed like the whole school was out there. I could almost picture their eyes wide with wonder.

I couldn't believe JJ had done it. Acting normal was one thing. Leaving me alone another. But hoisting himself up on the flagpole, for everyone to see? That took guts. He'd be in big trouble for sure. I almost had to admire him. JJ had a few screws loose, maybe more than a few, and he did plenty of things that made no sense at all. He had that awful wheeze, he smelled funny, he said weird things that bothered people. He was an expert at driving friends away. But I'll say this for him: JJ did what he set out to do, and he didn't care what others thought about it. He was true to himself. He was a kid, not a clone. You can't say that about everyone. Certainly not me.

"I'll see you later," I told Chloe, and slipped inside the school.

As the door closed behind me, I was surprised by the sudden hush. It wasn't dead quiet—I could hear the squawk and clamor of the kids outside—but it was as calm as I had ever heard it inside the school building. It sounded empty, or almost empty. As I walked down the hall, the *click-clack* from my cane-tip returned to me clean and clear. That in itself was a revelation. Usually those echoes were muffled and gummy, if not drowned beyond all recognition, by the dull roar of the middle-school herd.

I made my way down the hall, to the third door on the right, and stepped into the lobby of the main office. It too was quiet.

"Hello?" I called out.

No answer.

"Hello!" A little louder this time.

Still no answer. No answer, no sigh, no squeak of rolling

chairs on linoleum. No chunk and whirr of the copy machine. Then the front office phone rang. Two, three, five times. No answer.

I was alone in the office.

I walked to the counter and felt along it. I tapped a few times and stood still to listen to the echoes. I could tell there was a wall behind the counter, about ten feet away. To the left, an opening. Likely a doorway. I made my way around the counter and towards the spot where I thought I heard the opening.

I was right. An open doorway led to a back hallway. It was smaller than the main hall, the echoes tight and quick. The hall opened to my left and right. I could still hear the muffled excitement of the crowd outside. Then, an approaching siren. The fire department coming to save JJ.

I didn't have much time.

I crossed the hall and reached for the walls, feeling for a clue. I found a nameplate, a raised number, and then, *bingo*, braille. Probably my fingers were the first that had ever read those dots: *Teacher's Lounge*. I heard the soda machine humming in there, but no sign of any teachers.

I turned left, finding doors and signs along the way.

Data Manager.

Electrical Closet.

I reached the end of the hall and found a door with a sign that read *Bookkeeper*.

I crossed over and felt along the other side.

Supply Room.

I continued down the hall. I heard the siren shut off outside, and more men shouting over megaphones.

Then I found the bathrooms. *Faculty Men. Faculty Women.*

There was a mechanical whirr from somewhere outside. The firefighters raising a ladder? Surely my time was almost up.

I felt along the walls, searching for braille.

Assistant Principal.

Getting warmer.

I made my way around a small bench in the hall and felt the next door.

Principal.

Jackpot.

I gently checked the door handle. Unlocked. I opened it, as quietly as I could.

"Hello?"

I knew Mr. Zukowski was outside but couldn't be sure the room was empty.

"Hello?" I tried again.

No answer.

I heard the crowd cheering outside. Then Zukowski bellowing above them on his megaphone. Far away, through the hallway, the lobby, and out into the main hall, a slow rumble started.

The front doors! Kids were coming in the school, and with them, teachers. Janitors. The receptionist. The assistant principal. Zukowski. Everyone.

I swung my cane wildly around, searching for Zukowski's desk.

Thunk!

A quick pass of the hand confirmed I had found it.

The noises outside were growing louder now. I heard footsteps in the lobby.

I slung my backpack off my shoulder and unzipped it as fast as I could. I dug down deep, past my jacket, past my lunchbox, until I found Antonio. I pulled him out. When I felt his warm bumpy rubber butt, I couldn't help but smile.

I heard steps in the back hallway, close now. Someone putting change into the drink machine.

"So long, *mi amigo*," I said to Antonio. "You're Mr. Zukowski's problem now."

I placed him on the desk. A triumph. I took a second

to enjoy the accomplishment—*Maria Romero, putting a rubber chicken on the principal's desk!*—but only a second. I knew I had to scram. I zipped up my backpack and turned to leave.

Just then a voice stopped me cold.

"Maria!" exclaimed Ms. Griffin. I heard the *crick-pop-fizz* as she opened her soda can. "What brings you back here?"

"Oh, sorry, Ms. Griffin," I said, putting on my best poor-blind-girl voice. "I must have gotten turned around, what with all the noise and excitement."

"It's been quite a morning," she said.

"I'm afraid I'm a bit lost," I said. "Can you help me find Mr. Smith's room? I don't want to be late for roll call."

"Absolutely, Maria," Ms. Griffin said. "Follow me."

I didn't need to, of course. I knew exactly where Mr. Smith's room was. I knew every turn she was going to take, fifteen feet before she took it.

But Ms. Griffin didn't know that.

And that was fine with me.

19

Trouble

Forty-five minutes later, I was back in that hallway, plunked down in a seat outside of Mr. Zukowski's office. We were just going over our science vocabulary when word came over the intercom: *Mr. Smith, will you please send Maria Romero to the office?* My heart jumped into my throat. I had never been called to the principal's office in my life, never done anything but what I'd been told. And here I'd stepped out of line just once—just one tiny little time—and sure enough I had been caught.

I wasn't surprised. One thing about being blind is, you never know who's watching you. I thought I had been alone in that office—nobody made a peep—but I couldn't be sure. A custodian could have seen me, a receptionist, another kid. That's the way it is with me in public places: if you don't speak, squeak, wheeze, shuffle, or grunt, there's a good chance I won't know you're there. Which is why I try not to pick my nose anywhere but in my own room.

So someone had seen me, somehow, somewhere, and now I'd been called down to Zukowski's office. I was scared witless but determined not to show it. I pulled out Roxie, stood up just as straight as I could, and walked out the door to meet my fate.

When I got to the office, Betty Jo Huddleston, the assistant principal, greeted me in a voice that was, at best, half-warm. She invited me into her office for a "little chat." (I've been around the block enough times to know you should be very careful when an adult invites you for a "little chat." Something bad is on the way.) Mrs. Huddleston told me the school surveillance cameras had caught me on tape, snooping around the back hallways while everyone was outside watching JJ up on the pole. And while there wasn't a camera in Mr. Zukowski's office, she wondered if I had anything to do with a strange and rather unsettling item he found on his desk.

Cameras, I thought. Of course. Stupid me. I can't see them, it's true, but Mr. Torres told me a long time ago that just about everything you do these days is caught on camera, at least if you're in a public place. Which is another reason to be careful where you pick your nose.

Mrs. Huddleston said that my behavior that morning was strange indeed, and that Mr. Zukowski had some questions for me. She said that he wanted to talk to me about what in the world I was up to, but that he was a little busy right now with another matter. I was to sit and wait until Mr. Zukowski was ready for me.

I sat down on the tiny bench right outside Zukowski's door, the same bench Roxie had found not sixty minutes earlier. I sat there for maybe ten minutes, but it felt like ten hours. I was scared, with tiny tears in the back of my eyes. (Yes, blind people can cry. Or at least most of us can. I can cry for sure. Real tears right down my cheeks, just like in the movies. But at this moment, just now, I was trying my best not to.) So I sat there, holding back the tears, wondering what Zukowski would do to me, dreading the phone call I knew he'd make to my mom.

Mom.

Thinking about my mom was the worst. I couldn't believe I had let her down. She had it hard enough even when I was a good girl, even when I did everything perfectly. What would she think now?

I distracted myself by trying to catch snippets of the conversation inside, where Mr. Zukowski and JJ were rehashing the morning's events. Actually, to call it a conversation is a bit of a stretch. It was more of a one-sided shouting match. Zukowski was hot under the collar, that's for sure. Between his threats and questions and grousing I could barely hear JJ's responses. I can't be sure, but I'm pretty sure JJ compared himself to Icarus, the Greek hero who flew too close to the sun. I know for a fact he offered a brief rebuttal on the strength of reinforced steel cable versus common flagpole rope. I strained for, but didn't hear, my name. Likewise, I didn't hear any references to challenges or the Twinnoggin Detective Agency. That was a relief. Whatever else he said, JJ didn't sell me out. I had to give him credit for that.

About ten minutes later, the door opened and JJ came shuffling out. Things had gotten quieter towards the end—I hadn't heard a good shout since JJ asked if he could go back up on the flagpole on Valentine's Day to sing love songs to the staff. With a crown of glitter and a purple ukulele, of course.

JJ came out of the principal's door and shut it behind him—Zukowski was on the phone with someone from the newspaper—and shuffled into the hallway. Then I heard him stop.

"Maria!" he exclaimed. "What are you doing here?"

"Well..." I hesitated.

"Well what?"

I smiled, for the first time since I'd heard my name on the intercom. "Well...it seems Mr. Zukowski found a rubber chicken on his desk."

Something tells me JJ broke into a smile right then also.

"The brave Antonio?" JJ asked, as if he could hardly believe it.

"The brave Antonio," I confirmed.

JJ whistled softly "My, my, Maria. The second challenge. I didn't know you had it in you."

"I'm full of surprises."

"Well done."

"And you," I said. "Up on the pole."

"Up on the pole."

"What was it like up there?"

"Amazing. Best view in town," JJ said. "But Zukowski's not impressed."

"What did he give you?"

"Three days OSS." OSS was out-of-school suspension. JJ wouldn't be back until next Thursday.

"Not too bad," I said.

"I hope that's all it is."

"What do you mean?"

"After Zukowski gets off the phone with the *Bugle*, he's calling my mom."

"And?"

"And for all I know, I'm on my way to Marbletown Academy."

"The Academy?" JJ had told me before that his mom had threatened to send him there, but I didn't think it was for real. "Isn't that the school for, um, troubled kids?"

"Indeed. The dropouts, the hoodlums, the knife-fighters," JJ confirmed. "*Alternative Education*, they call it."

"You like alternatives," I said. "You know, zig when others—"

"Zag. Of course. But, Maria, there's alternative, and then there's *alternative*. I don't know if the Academy is the kind of alternative I'm looking for."

"Who knows? You might like it."

"Maria, those kids would make a hash of me. You think I've got it bad here? Just wait and see what that lot does to me."

He sounded genuinely scared. I was worried for him. "I'm sure there are some good kids there," I said.

"Some, sure," JJ said. "Not enough."

"Don't sell yourself short, JJ," I said. "You might surprise yourself."

"Maybe," he said.

"I think you'd be fine."

"Maybe."

"But I hope it doesn't happen," I heard myself saying. "I'd rather have you here."

That surprised me a little. But it's sure enough what I said.

"Thanks, Maria," he said.

JJ was still standing there. He wasn't ready to go back to class. He was scared. More scared, even, than I was. I reached my hand out towards him. He grasped my hand between his own.

"Thank you, Maria."

I could tell he was on the verge of tears. I didn't want him to cry. I didn't want to cry either. No tears at all would be fine with me, just fine.

"I've passed my second challenge," I said, doing my best to distract him from the trouble he was in. "What's next, Captain Munson?"

20

Zukowski

JJ didn't have time to answer before Mr. Zukowski opened his door and called me inside. I thought I was in for a lecture, a real spittle-spewing tongue-throttling along the lines of what JJ got. But Mr. Zukowski didn't seem angry with me. Mostly, he seemed perplexed.

"Why did you do it, Maria?" he kept asking.

He didn't ask me if I had done it. That much was beyond question. Yes, I had done it. Yes, that was me on camera. Yes, that was me sneaking around the back offices while everyone else was outside. Yes, indeed, that was me feeling my way around, reading the braille signs on all the doors, not stopping until I found his door. And, yes, that was me who put the rubber chicken on his desk.

So Mr. Zukowski didn't want to know *if* I had done it. He just wanted to know *why*.

"I don't know," I told him.

And that was the truth.

I certainly didn't wake up that day intending to put Antonio on Zukowski's desk. That was never part of the plan. I'd meant to take him out of my backpack at home last night, and leave him there. I'd just forgotten.

So what made me do it? What changed my mind? Was it finding out that JJ was up on top of the flagpole? (The flagpole! Of all the crazy things!)

Or was it the feeling, that new, new feeling, of being alone inside, all by myself, just me and the echoes of my cane in that empty hallway? Was it the *opportunity* that made me do it? I mean, think about it. A girl like me doesn't get the chance to be bad very often. What did it mean that I took the first chance I got?

"What made you do it?" Zukowski asked again.

"I don't know," I said again.

"Well, Maria, it's very odd, that's for sure. I can't claim to understand it. And it's a direct violation of school policy. You are not to be in my office unsupervised at any time."

"I'm sorry, Mr. Zukowski."

"You know, Maria, if it was anyone else, I'd put a letter of reprimand into their permanent file. That's the kind of letter that follows you to high school. But I'm not inclined to do that in your case."

I should have been relieved, I know. Instead, I felt insulted.

"Why not?" I asked. "Why not put a letter in my file?"

"Because."

"Because what?"

"It's just that, well, you know."

"What?" I challenged him. "Is it because I'm blind?"

"Well, I'd just hate it if, you know, this letter made things...I don't know...more difficult for you later."

"Is that right?" I asked him.

"Well, um," he stammered. "Yes. Sure."

I couldn't believe it. Mr. Zukowski, the big bad principal, brought to his knees at the thought of punishing a blind girl.

"You'd hate it worse if I grew up spoiled."

"What's that?"

"I said, you'd hate it worse if I grew up spoiled. If I thought I was too special to get punished. You're always preaching responsibility, right?"

"Well..."

"Do it."

"What's that?"

"Do it. Write me the letter. Don't treat me any different."

"Well now, Maria, that's up to me, isn't it?" I was glad to

hear a little edge back in his voice. "It's not your place to tell me what to do."

"Yes, sir," I said.

"Back to class with you, Maria," he said. He even sounded a little scary this time. *That's better*, I thought. He shouldn't be scared of me. I should be scared of him.

"Yes, sir," I said.

"And no more chickens," he said, his voice louder still.

"No, sir."

"You're dismissed."

I stood up, unfolded Roxie, and headed into the hallway.

"Oh, Maria?" Mr. Zukowski called after me.

"Yes?"

"I'll be putting that letter in your file this afternoon. And a copy home to your mother."

"Yes, sir," I said. I walked out of his office, punished, scolded, and as proud as I'd ever been in my life.

21

My Crabby-Abby Days Top Ten List of the Most

Annoying Things About Being Blind,

In No Particular Order,

Numbers 8 and 9

8. Your attention
9. Your pity

22

Things You Might Be Wondering, Part Four: What I Wish

There's a fourth question I get a lot, which I haven't answered yet. It's probably the one I get the most.

It's this: *Do you wish you could see?*

I've thought about this one a lot, and right now my answer is no, not really. Blind is all I've ever known. I don't even really understand what it would mean to see. I guess seeing means you can understand the world by noticing the way light reflects off stuff, and what color it is, and how far away it is, and what shape it is, and all that. Like how I can get information by how sound bounces back to me. But seeing has got to be just the coolest, because I can tell you guys think the world of it. It must be ten times more useful than hearing to you, because there's this whole world built on what you can see, but you guys don't spend much time at all just listening. So, I guess seeing must be pretty great, but I don't spend time wishing I could do it. I don't even know what I'd be wishing for. It's like asking a fish if he wishes he could fly.

People say, *Well, don't you just want to see your mother's face, just once?* And I say, um, okay, sure. I guess so. Because I can tell they think it would be terrible not to see your mother's face, and people want for me to want that. But I've never seen my mother's face, and barring some miracle I never will, and that's been okay for me up to now. I mean, I don't see how I could know her any better, or love her any more, just because I could *see her face*.

It's true. I've never seen a sunset, or fireworks, or a full moon, or my mother's face. But you know what?

I don't need to.

23

People, Not Piles

Monday morning I was called to the office again.

What did I do this time? I thought as I walked down to the office.

Antonio the Chicken was last week's news.

Was I in for another lecture? A suspension? An apology from Zukowski for treating me like a child?

But Zukowski wasn't even there. Instead, Mrs. Huddleston called me to the front desk and handed me a packet of papers in a manila envelope.

I opened the packet, thumbed through the papers. There was nothing there I could read.

"UPOs," I said.

"Pardon?"

"What's this?" I asked.

"Oh, sweetie, that's JJ's homework. Didn't anyone tell you? JJ's mom called and asked if you could bring home his assignments while he's out of school. Your mom said that would be fine."

I'm sure she did.

"So all I need to do is bring these papers to JJ?"

"If you don't mind."

That's another thing I've figured out about adults. When they say, *If you don't mind*, they don't mean it. They mean, *You will not mind. This is what you will do.*

"Sure thing," I said. "Happy to do it."

I brought the papers to JJ first thing after school. That in itself was a small triumph of persuasion: I had to remind Mom that I was a big enough girl to navigate a full forty yards of empty suburban sidewalk without her help. (Even so, she probably stood on the porch and watched.) I made it without incident and delivered JJ's homework. Ms. Munson invited me to stay for a snack with the family.

Mary Munson was polite enough, but I could tell she was preoccupied, probably with her son and how to deal with him. I nibbled on her famous lemon cookies and we chatted for a while. Ms. Munson was determined to talk about anything, anything at all, as long as it wasn't the least bit important. We discussed all sorts of mindless things: science homework, the unseasonably warm weather, the upcoming field trip to Silver Dollar City. What we didn't talk about was JJ's crazy stunt, his suspension, or what she was going to do with that odd, sloppy, scattered boy of hers.

Cynthia was there too. I heard her playing with her toys, stopping to flip her playing cards now and then—*flick flick flick*—but she didn't say anything. She never does.

I was halfway through my second lemon cookie when Ms. Munson stepped out of the room to take a phone call. As soon as she did, JJ grabbed my elbow. It startled me.

"Watch it, JJ!" I cried. "What have I told you about grabbing—"

"*Your third challenge—*" he hissed.

"Is to maintain full use of my right arm." I pulled free from his grasp. "Don't grab me like that. Roxie might just find a way to smack your shins."

"Sorry, Maria." He dropped his voice. "But I have to give you your third challenge."

I was apprehensive. I hoped it had nothing to do with rutabagas or rubber chickens. Or marmalade. Or baby hedgehogs. Or whatever strange thoughts were bouncing around in JJ's addled head today.

"You've got to find out if Mom's going to send me to the Academy," he said.

"Marbletown?"

"Marbletown."

"Do you think she's going to?"

"I don't know. She's threatening it again."

"And you don't want to go?" I asked. "Plenty of zig-zag there."

"Maria!" he hissed. "This is no time for joking."

I shrugged.

"She'll tell you anything," JJ said. "She thinks you're the sweetest, most innocent girl in Marble City."

I shrugged. "Maybe I am."

"Ha," he said flatly. "Ha. Ha."

I shrugged again.

"I know better that that, Maria. And I'm glad I do. Because right now, I need you to be the opposite of innocent. I need you to be devious. And I need you to find out what she's planning. Please."

Ms. Munson ended her call and I heard her walking back towards the room.

"And convince her to let me stay at Marble City Middle," JJ whispered. Then he switched to a louder tone. "Cynthia, would you like to head out to the trampoline?" he asked. "Get in a few bounces before *Clifford* comes on?"

She didn't say yes, but she must have let him know somehow, because the next thing I heard was JJ opening the back door, and Cynthia following behind him. "We'll be back in a few minutes, Maria," JJ said. "She never bounces long."

"But you don't need to leave," he added. "Why don't you stick around, have another of my mom's famous lemon cookies?"

"I don't think I could," I said. "Maybe I should be going."

"Are you sure?" JJ asked, alarmed. He sounded like a tiny desperate, muffled mouse. I let him twist there for a few seconds.

"But I will take a glass of water," I said. "If you don't mind. I can probably stay a few more minutes."

I could almost hear JJ grin. "Absolutely," he said. "Kitchen's on your right. The sink is just past the fridge, with glasses in the cupboard just above." I listened for the hum of the refrigerator and had a little map in my mind in no time. "Stove's across from the sink," JJ added. "But not to worry. It's not been on today."

"JJ dear, I'll get her water," Ms. Munson said.

"That's okay, Ms. Munson," I said. "I've got this. Your son gives good directions."

I grabbed a glass and filled it at the sink. The sound of the sloshing water rose in pitch as I filled my glass, and I stopped just before it overflowed. I took a sip. A perfect fill.

I turned to Ms. Munson. "That was quite a stunt JJ pulled yesterday," I said.

"I'll say."

"It was all anybody could talk about at school."

"I heard," she said.

"I wonder what got in his head?"

"Who can say?" Ms. Munson said. "I love that boy, but half the time I have no idea what he's thinking. The other half, I think I do. I'm not sure which half scares me more."

So at least Ms. Munson and I had something in common.

"I'm surprised he didn't kill himself, pulling that foolish stunt," she said.

"He said he knew what he was doing."

"I'm not sure JJ is the best judge of that."

"Maybe not," I said. We sat there for a moment, silently. Fretting.

"So what are you going to do about it?" I asked.

"Do?"

"In the books I read, boys get punished for stunts like that," I explained.

"I'm sure they do," she said. "I just don't know what I can do with JJ. I don't know what I can do that will reach him."

"He's worried you're going to send him to the Academy," I told her.

"Marbletown Academy? I've thought about it, that's for sure. I'm just not sure it's the place for him. He's a sweet boy, he really is. But if he messes up again, I might have to. I think it's the only thing that will get his attention." I hadn't expected this. She was confiding in me like I was an old friend. My mom says there's something about being with a blind kid that makes folks cut the rubbish and talk straight, but I don't know about that. I've seen plenty of fakes in my time.

"JJ needs to be at Marble City Middle," I said. I was surprised to hear myself say it.

"Do you think so?" Ms. Munson asked.

"It would be too normal without him," I said. "The world needs more weird."

She laughed at that. "Well, if that's the case, the Munson family is doing our part."

"The Romeros too," I assured her.

"I suppose that makes us good neighbors," she said.

I shrugged.

"Sometimes it's good to zig when others zag," I said.

Just then, JJ and Cynthia came rattling through the back door.

"Enough bouncing for today, Cynthia?" Ms. Munson asked.

Cynthia gave her playing card a flick or two. I took it to mean yes.

"I guess so," JJ said. "*Clifford* starts in five minutes."

"I suppose I should be going," I said. "Thanks for the lemon cookies, Ms. Munson. They were divine."

"You're welcome, Maria," she said. "And thanks for bringing over JJ's schoolwork. You saved me a trip. JJ, why don't you walk Maria home?"

"She doesn't need that, Mom," JJ said.

"I know that, JJ. But a friend can walk another friend home. People do it all the time. Whether they're blind or not."

"True," JJ said.

I stood up and headed for the door. I felt a grip on my elbow. I was about to fuss at JJ for grabbing me again when I realized it wasn't his grip. It was softer. The hands were smaller.

"Cynthia?" I asked.

"It looks like she wants to come with us," JJ said. "I think she's taken a liking to you. Maybe she's tired of having a smelly and spastic big bothersome brother and would rather have a kind and quiet sister instead. Is that right, Cynthia?"

Cynthia didn't answer.

"If so, I'll give her credit for good judgement," JJ continued. "In a world of loudmouths, she respects the ones who carry themselves with a little more serenity. Unfortunately, serenity's never been my strong suit. C'mon, Maria. Let's you and me and Cynthia take a stroll."

I liked that about JJ. He was gentle with Cynthia but not demeaning. She couldn't read, she didn't talk, and she couldn't be counted on to keep herself safe. But JJ didn't see her limits. Or if he did, he didn't focus on them. I never heard him treat her like a baby, or worse still, a pet. He treated her with respect.

Come to think of it, that's how he treats me too. Like an actual person. You'd be surprised how hard that is for some people.

I've said it before: most people just see me as *The Blind Girl*. Not Maria, not the sixth-grade scientist, not as a kid who has all sorts of interests and ideas and enthusiasms of her own. Just *The Blind Girl*. Like I'm nothing more than my label.

I get it.

Labels are easy.

Here's a secret: I put labels on people too. Hannah's a *snob*. Her boyfriend Dalton's a *dumb jock*. Sam's a *nerd*, and JJ's a *weirdo*. What can I say? The labels fit.

Mr. Torres hates that thinking.

Don't put your people in piles, Mr. Torres says. Before long, all you see is the pile, not the person.

So I'll give JJ credit for that too. He sees people. Not piles.

We walked down the street together, with me in the lead, Cynthia on my arm, and JJ right beside. The sun was shining. A bird trilled in the distance. A beautiful day.

"So," JJ asked when we got to my front stairs. "Learn anything?"

"Nothing definite," I told him. "Sounds like she's still deciding what to do."

JJ moaned.

"But I put a good word in for you," I said.

"You did?"

"I did. Told her we needed you at Marble City Middle."

"You did?"

"I did."

"You're the best, Maria."

"Does that mean I passed the third challenge?" I asked.

"With flying colors."

24

Chicken Pox

JJ came back to school on Thursday, and I was only half-surprised to find that I was glad to have him back. The kid was growing on me.

Not that I ever would admit as much in the halls of Marble City Middle. Nope, that was gonna have to be our secret. I didn't write the rules, I just lived by them, and to be linked in the popular imagination with JJ Munson was social suicide. I had no desire to be the Mustard Girl to his Mustard Boy. Rutabaga Girl was quite enough, thank you.

That might sound cold, but I didn't see another choice. My social standing was precarious at the moment, and I knew it. Jasmine and Kaitlyn had been nice to me lately, but Hannah was getting harder and harder to read. Maybe she was just swept up in Dumb Jock Dalton, and didn't have time for a girl like me. But whatever the case, her voice didn't sound as friendly as it had before. It was clipped. More dismissive.

Of course, she was all butterflies and sunshine when the teachers were around. If you judged her only by how she acted when adults were around, you'd have thought Hannah was my best friend. But I knew she wasn't. She barely showed interest in me when the teachers walked away.

Not that I expected her to be my best friend, not by a long shot. But Hannah had a million friends, and if I wanted to have any social standing at Marble City Middle, I needed to be one of them.

The way I see it, being popular is like the chicken pox, except a good chicken pox. Just being around it gives you a chance to catch a bit of it for yourself. It's contagious. Even if I didn't need Hannah, I still needed her approval, and I was less sure than ever that I had it.

I wondered what she really thought of me. It was probably all in my head, but I could almost swear that every time I came upon her she was just finishing a sentence that had *rutabaga* in it. Or *rubber chicken*. Or worse yet, *JJ*. Because if popularity is the good chicken pox, JJ is the cure.

So was I popular? Not likely.

But was I, at the very least, *not unpopular?*

I couldn't just ask my friends to find out. Popularity is funny like that. No matter how bad you want it, you can't act like you do. You have to act like it doesn't matter. You have to act like you're not trying, like it just comes natural.

I knew there were all sorts of ways to find out if you were popular, but most of them were unspoken. Oh sure, I could tell who sat with who at lunch, who had the most kids crowded around them at their locker, who hung out together on the weekends. But I missed some of the subtler cues: a raised eyebrow, a roll of the eyes, a look of boredom on someone's face. Did Hannah smile when she saw me? Did she seek me out? When she helped me out in math class, was she paying attention just to me? Or was she looking up every thirty seconds to see who was noticing that she was helping the blind girl? I wasn't sure.

I wished I could see and hear what was going on when I wasn't around. I wished I could be a fly on the wall. I wished I could be one of those hidden cameras like the one that caught me prowling around the office when JJ was on the flagpole, recording everything that happened in the halls of Marble City Middle without ever betraying my presence.

And then I realized: that's JJ. He'd told me before that the best thing about being unpopular is that nobody sees you. Oh, sure, if someone wants to find JJ to pick on him, to insult him, to make fun of him, they find him easy enough.

But other than that, he says, it's like he's a ghost, walking through the halls, unseen, unknown, invisible.

"I don't worry what they think about me," JJ told me once, talking about Hannah and the rest. "Because I know that, most of the time, they *aren't* thinking about me. I'm the last thing on their minds."

Which is just what I needed: someone they weren't thinking about. A blank, a snoop, a spy. A detective.

Without even realizing it, I had stumbled on JJ's fourth challenge: to find out what Hannah really thought of me.

25

Anchor

JJ accepted the challenge. He said after all those random challenges I'd given him—be normal, leave me alone, sit on a pole—he was grateful for something a little spicier. Some real detective work, he said. A job like this could help him earn his stripes.

I said, "We'll see what you find out. I'll give you until next Friday."

I didn't hear from him all week. He told me he'd gone deep undercover, in what he called *covert surveillance mode*. All he needed, he said, were open ears and the invisibility of the unpopular. And so he strolled by Hannah's locker a few more times than strictly necessary, sat closer to her at lunch than he was accustomed to, found reasons to sharpen his pencil when he sensed that dirt was being dished in Ms. Griffin's math class. Friday after school he came to me with a full report.

"Maria," he announced as he settled wetly into the wicker chair on my porch, "I have completed my fourth and final challenge."

"And?"

"I believe I have succeeded. I have found out what Hannah really thinks about you. Or at least what she says about you when you're not around."

"And?"

"Before we begin," JJ said, "I have one question: Are you sure, absolutely sure, that you want to know?"

"Why wouldn't I?"

"The wise ones tell us that some things are better left unknown, some words better left unsaid."

"Well, you can tell the wise ones that these things need to be known, and these words need to be said. Spill, JJ."

"Remember, Maria, these were her unguarded moments, moments she thought were private."

"You mean private like at her locker, in the gym, in front of the whole school? That's not private."

"Perhaps *confidential* is a better word. She didn't mean for me to hear. Or you."

"So what?"

"So are you sure you want to know?"

JJ was telling me that what I was about to hear would be painful. And that maybe I didn't want to hear it at all.

And maybe he was right. Maybe I didn't. Maybe I should never have sent him on this mission. Maybe it could only ever have ended badly. But it was too late for that. He had the news, and it wasn't good. I couldn't stand the thought of him knowing what she'd said, and me not knowing. Of her knowing what she said, and me not knowing. Of everyone in her group—Jasmine, Makayla, Kaitlyn—of them all knowing, and me being the one in the dark.

The truth hurts, JJ was telling me.

I can take it, I was telling him.

That's my style, remember? I want to know the *how* of things, the *why* of things. The trumpet sound, the circle round, the toast gets brown. And just what Hannah Anderson really thinks of me.

"Tell me," I said.

"Okay, I will," JJ said. He took a deep breath. "She doesn't like you. Or at least that's what she tells her friends. The words I heard weren't kind. *Weird. Random. Rutabaga. Freak.*"

"Freak?"

"She says it's a drag always having to help you. She says she wishes you could just be normal."

Not my choice, I thought. Then, a second later, *Not that there's anything so great about normal.*

"She didn't have kind words for me either," JJ said. "But I expected that. I have the luxury of not caring what she thinks."

"Must be nice."

"You do too. The world and I give you full permission not to care what she thinks."

"I'll work on it," I said.

"I'm sorry to bring you this news, Maria. I know it hurts."

I shrugged.

"I thought at first this challenge was a test of my skills as a spy," JJ said. "My capacity to gather information. My ability to go unnoticed. But I see now that it's a test of my courage."

"Your courage?"

"It takes courage to tell a friend something she does not want to hear."

"I hate her," I said.

"Don't bother," JJ said. "She's not worth hating."

"She is to me."

"She doesn't know what she's saying. She's too wrapped up in her own head, her own life, to really think about anyone else. She can't see things from your perspective."

"So?"

"So it's not permanent. She'll grow out of it."

"I hope she hurries up."

"Well."

"What makes you so sure? What makes you so sure she'll grow out of it?"

"I'm not," JJ admitted. "Some folks never do. But she's got a chance. Just keep being the best Maria you can be. That's all you can do. Maybe she'll come around."

JJ sounded like my mom. It's okay when my mom sounds like my mom. That's her job. But my friends? My friends should not sound like my mom.

Besides, it was nonsense. Hannah Anderson wasn't going to come around. She was born that way, and would always be that way, as far as I was concerned.

"Do you think she'll come around on you too?" I asked JJ.

"That's a taller order, I admit," JJ laughed. "But you seem to have done it."

Maybe so, I thought.

Probably so.

"I'm reaching out my hand now, Maria. Shake?"

I grasped JJ's hand. I held on for a few seconds, thinking about what I had learned. I thought about Hannah. I thought about JJ. I thought about the way I was feeling at that moment, which was terrible. I thought about courage, and my mom, and being a weirdo. I didn't know what to make of it all. I felt like a ship tossed on stormy seas.

The funny thing was, JJ's hand felt like an anchor.

26

I Didn't

I would like to tell you that I took JJ's advice, that I put Hannah and her harsh words behind me. That I realized they had no power to hurt me, unless I let them. I would like to tell you that I understood that she was under pressure too— to be pretty and popular and perfect—and that I knew that just because she sometimes said horrible things didn't mean that she was a horrible girl. I would like to tell you I took the opportunity to reach her, and teach her, and help her see the error of her ways. I would like to tell you that I am wise and calm beyond my years. I would like to tell you I did the right thing.

But I didn't.

I stewed and steamed and sulked all weekend. I cried a little bit too. My mom asked me what was wrong, but I wouldn't tell her. I didn't want her sighs. I didn't want her lectures. And I sure didn't want her pity.

Don't put your people in piles, Mr. Torres said. But at that point I didn't care. I was putting Hannah in a pile all right. The *Stuck-Up Popular Snob* pile. The *Mean Girl* pile. The *People I Hate* pile.

And if Mr. Torres didn't like that, he could boo-hoo-hoo all the way home, for all I cared. I wanted revenge.

Can I tell you something else I hate about being the blind girl? It's having to be perfect all the time. Mom says I can't do anything foolish, or stupid, like everyone else does, because then people will decide that they were right about me all along. They'll decide I'm just some helpless, weird blind kid who doesn't understand how the world works. I have to set a good example, my mom is always telling me. Be competent. Kind. Caring. An ambassador for blind kids everywhere. Always a smile on my face.

Well, you know what, Mom? Some days that's okay. Some days it's not.

27

My Crabby-Abby Days Top Ten List of the Most

Annoying Things About Being Blind,

In No Particular Order,

Number 10

The very last most upsetting one:

10. I have to be nice to everyone. I have to make a good impression on everybody. I'm an ambassador for the blind.

Puh-lease.

Ugh.

28

Little Maria

So, okay, we're out with it by now. You've figured out I'm not perfect. I can be crabby, mean, and spiteful. I sulk sometimes. I steam too. I do dumb things. Words hurt me.

Mom says there are two Marias inside of me. There's Big Maria, who is kind and caring and thoughtful, and who thinks about others before she thinks about herself. Then there's Little Maria, who is petty and proud and mean, who always thinks of herself first. She wants me to be Big Maria, of course. Just as often as I can.

But that weekend? That weekend, after JJ's news, I was Little Maria.

That weekend, I developed my plan for revenge. It would be short. Simple. Sweet.

I couldn't wait for Monday.

JJ's challenges had been difficult, in their way. They pushed me out of my comfort zone, made me try new things. But they were pointless.

To say *rutabaga* in class? Pointless.

To put a rubber chicken on Mr. Zukowski's desk? Pointless.

To find out if his mom was going to send him to the Academy? Okay, maybe that one had a point.

But my plan? It had a point too. A wonderful, devious, perfect, resentful point.

By the time I got to school on Monday, I was giddy with excitement. I ran into JJ in the hall before first period.

"I need you to sit near me during lunch," I said.

"Why's that?"

"You'll see."

"You got something up your sleeve?"

"My fourth challenge," I said.

"You can't give yourself a challenge. Only I can do that."

I shrugged. *We'll see.* I told JJ what else I needed from him, and exactly when I needed it to happen: 11:57. We even checked our phones to make sure we had the same time. Like real detectives.

"11:57," I reminded him as we split up. "On the dot."

"Got it," JJ said.

At lunchtime I asked Ms. Smitka, the cafeteria monitor, to find me a seat next to Hannah. When I'd first came to Marble City Middle, she'd told me she'd give me any help I needed in the lunchroom, anytime. I'd used her for the first week, while I figured out the layout of the room: where the lunch line was, where the milk coolers were, where my friends sat in the maze of tables. But I figured it all out pretty quickly, and hadn't asked for her help in months.

But today was no ordinary day. If my plan was to work, I needed to be sitting next to Hannah, and I wasn't above getting a little help to make that happen.

As she took me through the line, Ms. Smitka read me the menu choices, as she had during the first week of school. I played along, and let her read them, even though I knew full well what we were having. I'd looked it up online the night before and let VoiceOver tell me.

Chicken nuggets. Green beans. Pineapple tidbits. Banana pudding. Choice of milk.

And: mashed potatoes.

I got my lunch, and had Ms. Smitka guide me to a seat next to Hannah. I sat down, and waited. Hannah was sweet to me, just as I expected. She asked about my weekend, and if I was ready for the math test.

Faker, I thought.

I sat quietly, listening to the chit-chat of the table, stopping every few minutes to discreetly check the time on my phone.

I had the volume turned down to a whisper, so as not to raise suspicion. The topic for the day was which member of the boy band 4Real was the cutest. I voted for Trevor.

The time grew closer.

11:55.

11:56.

11:56 and thirty seconds.

Finally, 11:57.

If our plan worked, JJ would be rising from his spot at the adjacent table just now, walking towards the trash cans. Any minute I should hear a tremendous clatter...

CRASH!

Right on cue. JJ had tripped and dropped his tray on the cafeteria floor. Just as I had planned.

I heard the *whoosh* of a dozen heads turning to look at him, and then the louder ruckus as the room erupted into mock applause. When they saw that the sap who dropped his tray was JJ, the cheers grew even louder.

But I didn't turn. And I didn't clap. It was just the distraction I needed. I quickly slipped one of my fake eyes out of its socket, reached over, and tucked it on top of Hannah's mashed potatoes.

When Hannah was done cheering JJ's clumsiness, she turned back to her plate. And there she saw my eye, wedged into her potatoes, staring up at her, unblinking, as if in judgement.

Hannah screamed.

29

I Did the Doing

Revenge was mine!

It was short, it was sweet, it had a point. It felt just as good as I thought it would.

But you can guess where that stunt landed me. Back in the principal's office.

I sat in the hallway outside Mr. Zukowski's office, waiting to be called in. And although I was alone, I wasn't lonely. For company I had the memory of Hannah's scream, and the pandemonium that followed. Of course, the teachers had come right away and demanded to know who had done it. Hannah called me out, and I couldn't deny it: I was the only one in the school who even had a fake eye. And, of course, my right eye socket was conspicuously empty at the moment. And, of course, the eye staring up out of her potatoes was an *exact match* of the one still nestled in my left eye socket. If ever there was an open-and-shut case, this was it. I was the only suspect.

Ms. Smitka said, "Maria, we are headed straight to Mr. Zukowski's office."

"Yes, ma'am," I said. I stood up. "Hannah, would you be a darling and wrap my eye up in a napkin for me?"

"Excuse me?"

"I need my eye. The one in your potatoes, not the one in my head. Just wrap it up in a napkin, and I'll take it with me."

"Yes, of course," Hannah sputtered, then did as she was told. She fished my eye out of her potatoes, wrapped it up in a napkin, and handed it to me. One careful cleaning and it would be as good as new.

"All right, Ms. Smitka," I said, after shoving the napkin-wrapped eye in my pocket. "Let's go see Mr. Z."

As we walked out of the lunchroom I heard a rising tide of conversation. A roomful of sixth graders was still trying to make sense of what happened. They had heard the crash of JJ's tray, and they had heard Hannah scream. They had seen Hannah's friends gasp and throw their hands over their mouths, watched Ms. Smitka come storming over to the table. But it took them a while to piece it all together. When they figured out I was the culprit, I could almost hear their jaws drop. An excited murmur ran through the lunchroom, punctuated here and there by a few ripples of laughter, as the kids started talking about what I had done.

What came next, I wasn't sure. I was headed for trouble, I knew that much. Mr. Zukowski would not be pleased. Still, I smiled as I left the lunchroom.

For years, I had been *done for* and *done to*.

Today, I did the doing.

❧

As I waited for Mr. Z in the office, Mr. Torres walked in.

I had forgotten we had a make-up lesson scheduled right after lunch. It didn't look like that would be happening now.

"Maria!" he exclaimed. "Fancy meeting you here." Mr. Torres usually checked in at the office and had me called down to meet him. "To what do I owe this surprise?"

"It seems I've got a meeting with the Big Chief," I said.

"Zukowski?"

"That's the one."

"And how did that come about?"

"There was an incident in the lunchroom," I said.

"Zig-zag?"

"Zig-zag," I said.

"What happened?"

I told him.

"Maria, I'm surprised at you."

"The world needs more weird," I said.

"I'm all for a fiery and indomitable spirit, Maria. But you can't be putting your eyes in other people's potatoes."

"I know, Mr. Torres."

"Are you sorry you did it?"

"I haven't decided yet."

He paused. "Fair enough. I guess this means we won't be working together today?"

"You could ask Mr. Z., if you want. But I doubt it."

"It's a shame," Mr. Torres said. "You've been making good progress lately."

"Some things are starting to click," I said.

"It seems so," Mr. Torres agreed.

"So are you going to set me free soon?" I asked.

"Maria, we talked about this—"

"No, listen for a minute. You just said I'm getting better. I know where I am, most of the time. I know where I'm going. I've been getting good at listening to traffic. I can tell the difference between a stop sign and a traffic light. I can hear when traffic has a turn signal. I can tell the difference between a car going fifteen miles an hour and a car going forty. And it's been a long time since I wandered out into the middle of the street. I think I'm ready."

"Well—"

"Mom won't let me go until she hears from you, Mr. Torres. But I'm ready to leave the nest. Mr. Torres, it's time to let this birdie fly."

"Maria, you've made wonderful progress this year. I've said as much. But you're not quite ready. You're doing great, but you've got to be 100 percent."

"Ninety-nine and a half just won't do," I said.

"You know what happens when we make mistakes."

"Maria Pancakes," I said.

"Give us another six months. A year tops."

A year? I thought. *A year?* Adults always forget how long a year is to a kid. Maybe once you've had forty or fifty of them, they all seem to slide together. But I'm twelve. A year is still a pretty big deal. I didn't want to be led around like a puppy dog for another whole year. I wanted to go out on my own. It sure didn't look like that would be happening, not any time soon.

My friends who can see complain that their parents don't trust them, that they don't give them enough freedom, enough room to grow. They have no idea.

The meeting in Zukowski's office was about what you'd expect. A few exasperated sighs, an aggressive swivel or two in his heavy leather office chair, and at least one muttered *I don't understand.* He asked me *Why?* about three different ways. But he must have known why. If you spend enough time around middle schoolers, I think the *whys* must be obvious.

But his question was not simply *why:* it was *why you, why now,* and *why that?*

I knew my answers wouldn't satisfy him, so I didn't say anything. Mostly I just listened, and when I had a thought I kept it to myself.

When Mr. Zukowski told me we all have problems with our friends, but there were better ways to express yourself than putting your eye in someone's potatoes, I thought, *Maybe so. But none that are funnier.*

When he told me he hoped that this didn't become a pattern, me getting in trouble and being called to his office, I thought, *Me too. I hope I get better at not getting caught.*

When he told me he expected better from me, I just shrugged. *Maybe you should expect a little less.*

I'm not amazing.

I'm not perfect.

I'm not even that good.

Sometimes I like it that way.

In the end, I got three days of out-of-school suspension, the same that JJ got for his flagpole stunt. I took my punishment, thanked Mr. Zukowski, and headed back to class, face forward, chin up, ready for whatever came next.

30

Complicated

Mom didn't take the news too well. She didn't get angry. She rarely did. But it worried her. She was worried for her darling daughter, her perfect little girl, her budding young scientist, her future valedictorian, the Maria of her dreams.

And while I thought she would want to talk about all the things I had done wrong, mostly she just wanted to talk about all the things she had done wrong.

Had she raised me right?

Had she given me enough attention?

Had she given me enough love?

Yes, yes, and *yes* were the answers to those three questions, but I didn't say that out loud.

Why was I angry at Hannah?

Long story.

What could she have done to help me find friends, good friends, true friends?

Nothing.

Was I lonely? Was I sad?

Not really and *not often. Just the normal amount, I suppose.*

What would lead her daughter to put her eye in someone's mashed potatoes?

We've been over this, Mom.

She didn't yell. But she cried. She cried a lot.

I felt rotten. I tried to tell her it was a simple prank, that she was making too big a deal of it.

"I'll decide how big a deal to make of it, Maria," she said. "I will. Not you."

Scheming with JJ had been fun. Scaring Hannah a hoot. Mr. Zukowski's disappointment had rolled right off my back, and Mr. Torres had seemed almost proud of me. Three days off school? I could use the break. It had been a remarkable day, the only one like it in my life, and until now, I couldn't see the downside of it.

But breaking my mom's heart, even just a little bit? That was hard to take.

Maybe being the bad girl was a little more complicated than I thought.

And then Three Golden Questions came to my mind. The questions Mr. Torres asked me to recite during our Where & How lessons. He asked them again and again and again.

Did I know where I was?
Did I know where I was going?
Did I know how to get there?

All of a sudden, I wasn't so sure.

31

A Perfectly Normal Day

Mom left me at home alone the next day. She didn't want to, but she didn't have much choice. Since I was suspended, I couldn't go to school, but Mom couldn't afford to miss any work. It wasn't long ago that she'd decided she could leave me home alone for a whole hour while she went to the gym. She still couldn't imagine leaving me alone for a whole day. She called just about everyone she knew, trying to find someone who could sit with me. Her sister, JJ's mom, her best friend, and who knows who else? Her mechanic? Her hairdresser? The clerk at the Marble City Stop-n-Shop? But she couldn't find anyone to stay with me. I told her I would be fine, told her over and over again, and finally she relented.

We agreed that I would text her every two hours—at nine, eleven, one, three, and five—to let her know I was still alive. To assure her I hadn't burned down the house, run off with the circus, or fallen down the basement stairs. I was to go nowhere. I was not to answer the door for anybody, and I certainly couldn't set foot outside the house. And while I could fix myself a peanut butter sandwich, under no circumstances was I allowed to touch the stove. JJ would be by after school with my homework. Until then, I was to get caught up on my math assignments, write a letter to my grandparents, and listen to the first three chapters of *A Wrinkle in Time*. After I'd finished all that, I could watch TV, listen to music, whatever I wanted, just so long as I was safe.

So that's what I did. I caught up in math, wrote my grandparents, and listened to *A Wrinkle in Time*. I watched a few online videos, answered a few texts, and made a peanut butter sandwich. I didn't touch the oven. I didn't fall down the stairs. I didn't set foot outside. A perfectly normal day. Until four o'clock.

At four o'clock I was supposed to meet JJ and pick up my homework for the day. But he texted me at 3:30 and said he didn't want to leave Cynthia home alone, that she didn't seem herself today. Could I come over to get the work? I said sure.

Yes, it would be a step outside of the house.

Yes, I would *technically* be breaking Mom's rules.

But JJ lived right down the block, and I'd made that trip plenty of times, with Mom and without her. Besides, what Mom didn't know wouldn't hurt her.

A couple of minutes before four, I threw on my sneakers, grabbed Roxie, and walked down the front stairs and onto the sidewalk. I turned left, towards JJ's house. It was a beautiful day, one of those late autumn days filled with sunshine. I could smell the turning of the leaves and hear the fallen ones crackle under my feet. Soon the air would turn crisp. I got to JJ's front door and rang the bell.

I expected his usual friendly bombast, but instead he opened the door in a panic. "Maria!" he gasped. He was panting, flushed, out of breath. "Have you seen Cynthia?"

"What? Cynthia? No."

"Heard her, smelled her, anything?"

"No," I said. "Not a trace. What's going on, JJ?"

"She's missing. I can't find her."

"What?"

"She was right there, just a little bit ago. Watching *Clifford* on the couch, like she always does. I told you she was acting strange, but with *Clifford* on, I thought I was safe. She never leaves *Clifford*."

"And?"

"And I went back to my room, got on my laptop. I was online for, like, fifteen minutes, maybe twenty. I read a few tweets, played one game of Dragon Snaggin'. Maybe two. I came out five minutes ago, and I can't find her anywhere. She's not on the couch, not in her room, not on the trampoline. I don't know where she could be. She just disappeared."

"Could she have come out the front door?"

"No," said JJ. "I always lock the deadbolt. I don't think she knows how to work it."

I thought back. I hadn't heard the deadbolt slide when JJ opened the front door. I was sure of it. I rang the doorbell; he jerked the door open. No deadbolt. I told him so.

"What?"

"The deadbolt wasn't locked, JJ. I would have heard it."

"Are you sure?"

"Yes."

"So, you're saying she unlocked the deadbolt for the first time in her life and waltzed right out the front door?"

"I'm saying the front door was unlocked, JJ. That's all I know."

He pushed past me and ran down the steps to the sidewalk.

"Cynthia!" he yelled.

He looked up and down the street.

"I can't see her!" he screamed. "She's gone. Oh god. Oh dear god. Mom is going to kill me. She is going to kill me dead, and then send my dead body to the Academy for the rest of middle school. But I don't care if she does, as long as we get Cynthia back. Maria, I've got to go," JJ panted. "I've got to find her. See you later."

"Wait!" I cried.

"What?"

"I'm coming with you."

32

Credit

Give JJ credit.

    He didn't say, *What?*

    He didn't say, *Why?*

    He didn't say, *But you're blind!*

    I'd heard all of those things before. Sometimes all three from the same person at the same time.

    Instead, JJ said, "C'mon, then. Time's wasting."

33

Trust

That's how I ended up looking for Cynthia. I said, *I'm coming*, and JJ didn't say no.

Ninety-nine out of one hundred other people would have said no.

JJ didn't.

I grabbed his elbow. I didn't know where we were going, and I didn't want to slow him down. He had eyes that worked. I didn't. He could do the navigating this time. Speed trumps pride when you're looking for a lost little girl.

Still, I held onto Roxie. It was an act of self-preservation, really. JJ was hardly the model of calm consistency. He was easily flustered, even in the best of times. And at this particular moment he was half out of breath, highly confused, and in a state of panic. Not the best time to trust him completely. So even though I had a firm grip on his elbow, I kept Roxie out in front of me, sweeping side to side like the sentinel that she is, on the lookout for any stray street signs, potholes, or mailboxes JJ was too agitated to notice. We got down the road at a pretty good clip.

"Where are we going?" I asked.

"Out to Washington," he said. Washington Lane. The main road at the end of our block.

"The library and the bakery are her two favorite places on earth," JJ said. "My guess is she's trying to find one of them. Probably the library. I'm hoping when we get out to Washington we'll just see her. Maybe she'll be there on the sidewalk, looking around. Or maybe she'll have sat down in the grass to look at some leaves. Who knows? With a twenty-minute head start, she could be anywhere."

"Did you call your mom?" I asked.

"Not yet. Let's get out to Washington and see if we can find her. Get her home safe and happy, plop her on the couch and give her a cookie. All before Mom gets home. She'll never have to know. That way she won't have to kill me or send me to the Academy."

"JJ, I think she should know."

"Give me one more minute, Maria." JJ quickened his pace a bit. We were practically running. I lifted Roxie's tip off the ground and let her skim just above the sidewalk. We were getting close to Washington, that much I could hear. The traffic noise was getting heavier.

We reached Washington and JJ stopped and looked both ways.

"She's not here, Maria. I can't see her anywhere. Oh no. Oh no. Oh, *please, please, please,* let me find her. She's not here, Maria." JJ seemed to be losing it. "What do we do next, Maria?"

"Which way's the bakery?" I asked.

"Left," he said, "three blocks."

"And the library?"

"Right. Two blocks."

"So she could have gone either way?"

"She could have gone either way," JJ agreed. "Oh no. Oh no."

"I guess we're splitting up then," I said.

JJ paused. "What?"

"I guess we're splitting up."

"Are you sure?"

"It only makes sense. We've got to find her. You call your mom and head for the library. You said that's probably where she is. I'll head to the bakery, just in case. We know she has a sweet tooth."

"But Mr. Torres—"

"Mr. Torres isn't here, is he?" Mom wasn't here, Mr. Torres wasn't here. This one was up to me and JJ.

Good students make good decisions, Mr. Torres often told me. *The trick is knowing what the good decision is.*

And what if you don't know? I would ask him.

You won't. Not always.

And then?

And then you trust yourself. You stop, think, and decide. And trust you made a good decision.

Well, I had stopped, and I had thought. And I had decided: JJ and I were splitting up. I was heading off to look for Cynthia. On my own. It was my decision. Not JJ's. Not Mom's. Not Mr. Torres's.

Mine.

I just hoped it was a good one.

I turned and walked off as if I had all the confidence in the world, but the truth is, I was scared witless. I'd begged Mr. Torres for this chance just yesterday. The chance to walk alone, blocks from home, with no adult to look over me. And now that I had it, I wasn't sure I was ready.

It didn't help that we had a real emergency on our hands. I mean, think about it: me and Cynthia, both of us out alone in Marble City for the first time. Me looking for her. Her not knowing I was even looking, maybe not even knowing she was lost. Not quite the way our parents imagined it.

Of course, I had it easier than Cynthia. If I ran into trouble, at least I could talk to someone. I could use my words, explain myself, make myself understood. I could ask for help when I needed it, get the lay of the land, use my phone if it came to that. Cynthia didn't have that option. There's no telling what she was thinking right now or doing. Or if she was safe. Or if she would remain so.

All of a sudden it seemed like a lot to take on. Worrying about myself seemed quite enough, thank you. Now I was worried about Cynthia too.

At the same time, I knew I had to stay calm. If I didn't think straight, I didn't have a chance. It wasn't my cane that was going to get me out of this one; it was my brain. If ever there was a time for reason and rigor, this was it.

I went back to Mr. Torres's three questions.

Did I know where I was?

Did I know where I was going?

Did I know how to get there?

I knew where I was: the corner of Franklin and Washington.

I knew where I was going: the Westside Bakery. *Three blocks away*, JJ had said. *On the left.*

It was the *how* part that worried me. I knew where I was, sure, and I knew where I was going. I just didn't know if I could get from here to there. But it was time to find out.

"All right, Roxie," I said. "Let's get this thing done." I swung my cane out in front of me and started walking.

34

Pumpernickel, Pomegranate, Persimmon

The first block was no problem. A straight sidewalk, with grass on the left and a curb on the right. I felt a few driveway cuts along the way, and Roxie found a telephone pole or two—thanks, old gal—but nothing I couldn't handle. As I walked I made sure to notice what was around me. I listened to the cars along Washington. They were going at a decent clip, but not highway speeds. Maybe thirty miles an hour, maybe a little more. It sounded like four lanes, two in each direction. There were gaps in the traffic noise now and then, but not many—we were getting close to rush hour. A busy road, a busy time.

I made note of a few landmarks, clues I could use to find my way back if I needed to. Kind of like Hansel and Gretel's breadcrumbs, if you've ever read that story. There was a low brick wall halfway down the block, and just after that a patch of broken sidewalk where the roots of a shade tree had pushed the concrete into a small peak. A dozen paces past that, there was gravel on the sidewalk. A quick sweep with Roxie confirmed a gravel driveway to my left, likely leading to some nice old house like the kind that you usually found in neighborhoods like this, where the houses were set far back from the street and the big leafy trees were large and mature.

It was four o'clock on a fall afternoon, and the sun hung in the western sky. It shone on the back of my neck, which told me I was heading east. I'd need to turn and face it to find my way back home. If the sun went behind the clouds, I'd use the grass: if it was on my left on the way there, I'd need it on the right on the way back.

The sidewalk sloped down, and I knew I was nearing an intersection. I swept Roxie side to side, looking for a ramp, or maybe one of those plastic panels full of bumps that the good people down at the street department are starting to install in sidewalks so people like me know when we're approaching a road. (*Giant Legos*, Mr. Torres calls them. Sam calls them *Street Braille*. I just call them sidewalk bumps.) But there were no sidewalk bumps to find; the street crew hadn't put them in here yet. Instead, I found a short ramp and a half-inch drop where the sidewalk met asphalt: not much, but enough to let me know I was at a cross street. It was time to stop and listen.

I've listened to a lot of traffic in my life, and believe me, I know. *Listening to traffic* sounds like about the most boring thing either of us can think of. Like *watching the grass grow* or *counting all the stones in the sea*. But I do it, and I'll continue to do it, because when I'm walking near cars, I want to know *where they are* and *where they are going*. Because, as I may have mentioned once or twice, I don't want to make Maria Pancakes.

Here's what I heard, and what it told me: the traffic on Washington ran nonstop, in a continuous flow, so I knew right away that there was not a stop sign for the cars on Washington. Because *none of them stopped*. Genius, right? So that meant that either the cars were all cruising through a green light (Option A), or that there was no traffic light, and the cars on Washington could just keep going and going and going until the cows came home, and then keep going after that (Option B). I know this stuff is easy when you can see it, but believe me, it takes some serious concentration when you're doing it with your ears.

I turned my attention to the street that ran into Washington, which was right in front of me. What street was it? I didn't know. I went to pull out my phone and ask it, *Where in the heck am I?* (Phones can't do everything, but they are *really good* at telling you where you are.) And that's when I realized I had left my phone at home, since I was only going to JJ's for a few minutes to get my homework.

Which is why I could almost hear Mr. Torres saying, *You shouldn't rely on your phone. It might not always be there.*

I could have waited for someone to ask—*what street is this?*—but I decided it didn't really matter. I decided a long time ago that if I didn't know the name of a street I was standing in front of, I'd give it one. It would help me remember it better the next time I found myself there. So I decided to call this one Pumpernickel Boulevard. I told myself I was standing at the corner of Washington and Pumpernickel.

Just then, a car pulled up on Pumpernickel, right in front of me, and came to a stop. It sat and idled for ten or fifteen seconds, and then took advantage of a break in traffic on Washington to turn left. It wasn't a long break, but it must have been long enough, because I didn't hear any tires screeching, and I definitely didn't hear a car crash.

I had all the clues I needed. We had a stop sign on Pumpernickel, and no sign or light on Washington. The time for me to cross would be when there was a steady flow of traffic in the lane nearest to me on Washington, moving forward, not slowing to turn.

I put my cane in the ready position, checked the traffic once more, and stepped into the street, making sure to walk just as straight as I could. I was about halfway across when I realized something: I had never done this before. I had never crossed a street by myself. Mr. Torres was always there. Or Mom. Or in a couple of cases my grandparents. Today, there was nobody with me, no one here to stop me if I made a bad decision, if I stepped out into the street just as a car turned onto Pumpernickel, or lost my bearing and walked into the oncoming traffic. No one to say "Stop!" or put a hand on my shoulder. I was doing this alone. The bird had flown.

I felt the road dip toward the gutter, and Roxie quickly

found the curb. I stepped up onto the sidewalk. A successful street crossing. All alone. No pancakes. Score one for Maria. I continued east on Washington. The next block was uneventful. One low-hanging branch did reach out and swipe across my face, but it was a glancing blow, a minor scratch. No blood, no foul. No big deal. Roxie's great but she can't find tree limbs.

I reached the next cross street and stopped to listen. It was another street I'd never encountered before, so I named it Pomegranate. It sounded like the last intersection: Washington didn't stop, and Pomegranate seemed to have a stop sign. I waited a bit longer, listened again to confirm my impressions. I was right, I was sure of it. I stepped out when I heard a steady stream of traffic running parallel to me, and just then a pickup truck turned right into my path. I had a split-second to react or it would be pancake time for sure. I froze. The truck whipped by, close enough for me to feel a breeze on my face. But it didn't hit me. I shuddered just a bit, caught my breath, and finished crossing the street. Two for two wasn't bad, but that hadn't felt near as good as Pumpernickel. I'd almost gotten killed.

Still, two for two was better than one for two, and I had places to go. I picked up my pace. The next block was shorter, and up ahead I heard more traffic, a larger intersection. I reached the edge of the sidewalk and started my analysis. It was a bigger street than the last two. It sounded like four lanes in each direction. I decided I would call it Persimmon.

As I stood listening, I heard the cars on Washington slow and come to a stop—most likely for a red light. A moment later I heard a surge of traffic on Persimmon, and then a steady flow, running right in front of me. I stayed a couple of steps back while I listened. The traffic was moving left to right at a pretty good clip. Wander into Persimmon now, and I'd be toast for sure.

Meanwhile, the cars on Washington idled patiently, with

more of them arriving at the intersection every few seconds. There had to be twenty of them.

After a half a minute, the traffic on Persimmon slowed and stopped, and a heartbeat later, the traffic on Washington rumbled to life, a surge of engine noise as the cars parallel to me accelerated from a standstill up to fifteen miles an hour, twenty, thirty. The pattern was unmistakable: I was at a traffic light, with cars coming from all four directions.

It was the largest street of the three I had found, and the most dangerous. Dozens of cars were coming through each change of the light, moving at a pretty good clip like I said, every driver safe inside their steel-wheeled pod, aiming down the road in a half-trance, thinking more about their destination than what lay in front of them. They had plenty of distractions too: the radio blaring; their cellphones, of course; perhaps a toddler in the backseat, wailing because he'd dropped his binky.

Drivers aren't monsters, Mr. Torres always said. They don't want to run over a blind girl. No one does. They're good, caring people, who are just trying to get to their next stop safely. But sometimes they can get a little distracted. Never assume you have their attention; never assume they'll see you; never assume they'll stop.

I felt my courage slip. I'd only crossed two streets, and the second one just barely. Maybe it was better just to turn around and head home. Maybe it was someone else's job to find Cynthia. Maybe JJ had already found her.

Then I thought of something else Mr. Torres always said: *Don't let fear paralyze you*. There is risk in crossing streets, just as there is risk in everything we do. The only way to eliminate all risk is to bolt your butt to the couch, never leave your house, never live a life.

And that never sounded like a trade I wanted to make.

I did not want to be paralyzed by fear, and I did not want to turn back.

The only option left was to go forward.

I faced Persimmon, lifted my chin, listened in once more, and confirmed that I was at a traffic light.

I waited. A half minute later, Persimmon slowed and stopped—the circle round, the trumpet sound—and there was a heartbeat's pause before Washington surged to life. When I heard that surge, I swung Roxie out into the street and started walking. Halfway across, an oncoming car took a right turn onto Persimmon, cutting right in front of me. A little too close for my taste, but this time I was ready: I heard their tires slow as they got ready to turn, and so I slowed just a bit myself, giving them the time and space to roll right in front of me. Then I walked on. I felt Washington dip and I widened Roxie's arc, searching for the curb. I found it and stepped up onto the sidewalk. Three for three.

35

Not Lost

I had to be getting close. JJ said the bakery was three blocks away, and I'd covered three blocks. I had crossed Pumpernickel, Pomegranate, and Persimmon. The sidewalk was wider here, but more crowded too. Roxie took the brunt of it. She banged and clanged against all sorts of things: lampposts, bike racks, bus stops. There were tables strewn about, and chairs by those tables, and sandwich-board signs propped up on the sidewalk, telling the world about the wonders that awaited those that stepped inside. (Mom has read them to me before. *Pumpkin Spice Lattes. Bubble Tea. Shrimp and Grits* on special.) I had moved on from the green grass and shade trees of the neighborhood to a more bustling, businessy place. All the more reason to stay alert.

When I was young, these bustling businessy places used to confound me, with all the new and novel things to whack with my cane. (*Street furniture*, Mr. Torres called them. *Clutter*, I responded.) I would hit things on my right, and then things on my left, and before long I was junebugging from one side of the sidewalk to the other, not moving forward so much as moving away from whatever I had collided with last. Mr. Torres suggested I take a middle path and try to avoid the mess altogether. It's not as easy as you might think.

After a solid run of chairs, tables, and signs, Roxie found a metal grate, followed by a soft thwack of wood. That's how I discovered they had planted trees on this stretch of Washington Avenue, to make it ever more lovely and serene. Don't get me wrong: I love trees. There was a time in third grade when I considered two cherry trees on Franklin Street better friends than most of the people I had met. But while I expect trees in lawns, and I expect trees in forests, I still don't expect them smack dab in the middle of sidewalks. But Roxie found the tree anyway. (Score another point for Roxie: She doesn't worry about where things *should be*. She just reports where they *are*.) I stepped around the tree.

While Roxie was busy with her work, my ears were busy too. I heard buildings to my left, close by, probably within ten feet. Big brick buildings, I guessed, considering the way my cane taps came back to me—short and sharp—and the way more distant sounds were blocked in that direction. I stepped toward the buildings to give a closer listen. The echoes grew sharper, suggesting a row of plate-glass windows, and as I walked, I heard that the brick and glass were punctuated now and then by a recessed doorway. Above each doorway, I heard the air above me grow smaller and softer, the bright distant forever of the sky giving way to a tent-like embrace: awnings, spread above the windows to protect from the rain and sun.

I counted three doorways, and three awnings, all on the left. One of them was probably the bakery. I doubled back and checked the door closest to Persimmon. I yanked it open and poked my head in.

I smelled talc and shampoo, with a touch of liniment and the acrid tang of a curling iron. *Hair salon.* Quick scissor snips confirmed my guess, and a moment later a hair dryer whirred to life, just in case I'd missed the first four clues. I closed the door and moved on.

I walked to the next door. A heavier door this time, and one that opened with a jangle of bells. It was warmer inside than the hair salon, both in temperature and sound. There were soft surfaces all around, swallowing Roxie's taps. A muted violin concerto played overhead. The smell here was more linseed oil and new upholstery. It wasn't crowded. I listened for footfalls, but heard none. My cane hit the side of a chair, and I reached for it. It was covered in smooth leather, and rocked beneath my grip.

"Can I help you?" a friendly female voice called out.

"Yes, actually, you can," I answered. "Where am I?"

"You're in Foothills Home Furniture," she replied.

"Foothills Home Furniture?"

"That's right. We sell couches, chairs, tables, dressers, rockers, recliners, ottomans. Anything you'd like to sit on, or set something up upon, we've got it. Could I help you find something?"

Cynthia, I thought. *You could help me find Cynthia.*

But what I said was, "No thanks."

"I'm not shopping today," I added. "Just taking the lay of the land. Thanks for your help."

"No problem, dearie."

I ducked out and continued east. I clattered past the tables and chairs I had hit before, and side-swiped a sandwich board too. It probably said something about the soup of the day, but I'll never know. This had to be the bakery. I eased around the sandwich board, found a welcome mat with my cane, and opened the door for a closer look.

I knew right away I'd found my spot. The smells hit me first: fresh ground coffee, cinnamon and vanilla, a whiff of ginger and molasses mixed in. A whole lot better than the hair salon.

There were lots of sounds, too, a whole pile of them, a regular symphony. I stepped inside and stood there for a moment, listening, trying to sort out all those sounds, to separate the signal from the noise.

There were plenty of people inside, making plenty of noise, and most of the sounds I heard were people sounds. I heard five or six conversations at once, from the breezy banter of sports fans to the oblivious bray of a businessman on a cellphone to the hushed mutterings of a couple cooing quietly in the corner. Even louder than the conversations were the barks of the wait staff:

For here or to go?

Order up!

Tall lowfat caramel latte!

Beneath all that chatter was a cacophony of common coffeeshop sounds: the clink of forks and knives on porcelain, the rustle of paper bags at the register, the manic shudder of the automatic bread-slicer doing its work. From a corner behind the counter, I heard a barista working on a latte: the heavy clunk of the filter handle, the watery dribble of espresso, and finally the dull roar of the steamer, rising in pitch as the milk gained air and grew thinner.

Above all that, there was a speaker playing jazz saxophone in 5/4 time.

And those were just the obvious sounds, the ones you could hear without even trying.

But there were subtler sounds, ones that could sink below the surface if you weren't paying attention. The screech of a chair pushed back over linoleum tile, the jangle of a handful of change tossed into a tip jar, the soft flick of a playing card, the gentle swoosh of a turned newspaper page.

The soft flick of a playing card?

I did my best to ignore the symphony and homed in on that singular sound. A card game has a recognizable rhythm: the flutter of the shuffle, the *chk-chk-chk* of the deal, the almost silent sorting of cards in the hand. This sound was different. Rhythmic, repetitive. *Flick-flick-flick.* Like a card in bicycle spokes. Or a card slipped over fingertips, again and again.

Cynthia!

I rushed toward the sound, abandoning all care, careening off a line of waiting customers and nearly tripping over a chair pushed out too far into the aisle.

"Cynthia?" I asked in the direction of the sound.

No answer.

Flick-flick-flick.

The sound was closer now. I slowed down, edging forward, until I found the table where it came from.

"Cynthia?"

Still no answer.

Flick.

There was someone there, I could tell. It was someone smaller than me, I could hear that much. But I couldn't be sure it was Cynthia. For all I knew, I was speaking to some terrified toddler, left to his own devices by a harried mom while she was adding a little cream to her coffee. I thought it was Cynthia. But I didn't know.

I could have asked someone in the room, of course. *I'm looking for a girl named Cynthia, about seven years old. I'm told she has blonde hair. She might be holding a playing card.*

But if I did that it would cause a scene for sure: a blind girl, lost, looking for a lost girl, mute.

It wouldn't do.

Besides, I wasn't lost.

I took a chance.

"Cynthia," I began. "It's Maria."

Flick-flick.

"It's good to see you too. I knew I'd find you."

Flick.

"But we've got to go now. Your brother is looking for you. Your mother too."

Flick-flick.

"It's time, Cynthia. Time to go."

I heard the scoot of a chair, and then a hand grabbed my arm, just above the elbow. It was a small hand, familiar. I could hear someone breathing, quiet, holding on. Waiting to be led.

"Good girl, Cynthia," I said. "Let's go."

36

Home

It wasn't hard getting home. The trip home is always easier than the trip out, at least if you were paying attention. I knew where the front door to the bakery was, and I knew I'd turn right when I got out of it and onto the street. After that, I knew I'd pass the furniture store and the hair salon, and after that the building would end and the sounds of Persimmon Street would open up.

There would be three intersections—Persimmon, Pomegranate, Pumpernickel—the first controlled by a traffic light and the other two by stop signs. Between Pomegranate and Pumpernickel, there would be a tree branch hanging down, which would not scrape my face this time, because I'd be ready for it. After Pumpernickel, I'd find a gravel driveway and a stone wall, and then I'd be close to Franklin. Then a right turn and we'd be home. Easy-peasy. No problemo.

Still I stopped at every corner, paying attention, listening close. I knew what I was listening for, of course, but I wanted to know it again, to make double-sure. There would be no Maria pancakes, and no Cynthia pancakes either. I crossed when the traffic ran parallel to me, on the lookout for turning cars and stray pedestrians. I crossed all three streets without incident. (Six for six, if you're scoring at home.) As I walked, I swept Roxie wider than usual, knowing that I needed space for two now: myself and Cynthia. If I didn't want a stop sign in my face, I figured she didn't either.

I found my landmarks—tree limb, gravel drive, stone wall—and when I hit Franklin, I took a right. We were home free.

We had walked in silence until then—I was busy listening to traffic, after all, and Cynthia doesn't speak—but once we were back on familiar turf, I started talking a blue streak. It was small talk, nothing of consequence, but I hardly shut up all the way home. I guess I was relieved, and that relief turned into a nonstop flood of words. I told Cynthia what I had heard and what we had done, how I had found her and how we were heading home. I talked about the rustle of leaves underfoot, the distant sounds of Washington Avenue, and the lonely song of a sparrow in the trees above us. I talked about the sound of waterfalls, the taste of tangerines, and the smell of rain on hot pavement.

I don't know if she understood—or even if she was listening—but I hoped it would comfort her. I know it comforted me. Besides, when two people are walking down the street together, and not having to listen for every car, bike, and moped, I think they should talk. Even if those two people are me and Cynthia.

We couldn't have been more than fifty yards from home when they found us. It surprises me now to say it, but I hardly heard them coming. It's not often I miss the sound of a squad car rushing up behind me, its big V-8 engine thrumming with all the purpose and precision a cop car can muster. But that's what happened, followed by a short squeal of tires and a car door opening.

Next I heard a scream of relief.

"Cynthia!"

It was Mary Munson. She sounded terrified. Joyous and terrified. Joyous, terrified, and relieved. She rushed over and embraced her daughter.

"Cynthia, Cynthia, I've been so worried!" She gave Cynthia a hug then, a big hug, a long hug, a shoulders-shuddering big long hug. She began to sob. I felt Cynthia's grip loosen on my arm, and then let go as she returned her mother's hug. I stepped to the side.

The rear door to the cruiser opened, and I heard footsteps approach. Then the breathing. Wet, wheezy. Was that mustard I smelled?

I felt a hand on my shoulder.

"Nice work, Maria," JJ said. "I knew you could do it."

37

Just Maria

There were an awful lot of tears before anyone spoke. For being so happy, Mary Munson sure did cry a lot. I guess I can't blame her.

It took Ms. Munson a while to sort out what had happened, particularly since JJ was being a little cagey with some of the details. But soon enough she had sorted it out: Cynthia had wandered off, unattended, and JJ and I had set out to find her. When we reached Washington, we had split up: me to the left, JJ to the right. When Ms. Munson figured out that I was the one who found Cynthia—out on my own for the first time, finding my way and finding her child—she was flabbergasted. She had me recount the details, all the details, and paced back and forth as I told her.

"You're amazing!" she cried when I finished.

"Not amazing," said JJ. "Just Maria."

Once Ms. Munson had caught her breath, gotten all hugged out, and heard the whole story twice more, she took Cynthia's hand. "Come on, dear," she said. "Let's go home now."

"Excuse me," I said. "Ms. Munson?"

"Yes?"

"Well, this might sound kind of weird, but I wonder if I could walk Cynthia home. You know, finish what I started."

"Walk her home?"

"That's right. We can't be more than fifty yards away, right?"

"About that."

"And, well, it's like this: I set out to find Cynthia and bring her home. And I found Cynthia. And I brought her most of the way home. And now I want to finish the job."

"Of course," Ms. Munson said. "Do you mind if I walk with you?"

"Not at all. Come on, Cynthia," I said, offering my arm. She grabbed on, just above the elbow.

I walked her home.

Just as we arrived, Ms. Munson's phone pinged with a text from my mom. I'd missed the five o'clock check-in. She must have been worried sick.

Ms. Munson read the text to me: *Have you seen Maria? I haven't heard from her since three.*

She texted back: *She's here. Safe and sound.*

There? With you? What happened?

Long story.

I'm on my way.

Mom got there in five minutes flat, and of course I had to tell her what had happened. After she'd heard the one-minute version, she wanted to hear the five-minute version. After she heard that, she wanted to hear *everything*, the whole tale, the thirty-minute soap opera.

"Do we have time for that?" I asked.

It turned out we did, because the Munsons invited us to stay for pizza, the better to sit around and sort it all out. We got a couple of cheese pies and made an evening of it. JJ told about how the afternoon had gone, about Cynthia not seeming herself, about his growing panic when he realized she wasn't at home. He told about the deadbolt, our trip down Franklin together, our decision to split up. He didn't find her at the library, of course, and that's when he called his mom.

Then it was my turn. I told the story of how I walked to the bakery and found Cynthia. I threw in a few details I knew they'd like—the sounds of the stoplight at Persimmon, the *flick* of the playing card that led me to Cynthia—but I asked them not to make too big a fuss. I had walked three blocks by myself and found who I was looking for. Like any other twelve-year-old could do. No big deal, no big fuss, not amazing. Just Maria.

Mom and Ms. Munson ate up the story, even at the third telling. We were both due for a scolding—JJ for losing track of Cynthia, and me for leaving the house without permission—but I could tell their hearts weren't in it, not today. They were just happy we were all home and safe. The scoldings could wait.

As Mom and Ms. Munson chatted over a plate of lemon cookies, JJ invited me to the backyard. Cynthia was on the trampoline now, and he said he didn't want to let her out of his sight again, not for a good long while.

"Well, Maria, we have done it," JJ announced when we got into the yard.

"Indeed, we have."

"We are done."

"Done," I said.

"Our task is completed, our mission finished, our race run."

"Our race is run."

"Some weeks ago we set out a series of challenges to determine if we had the valor, the virtue, and the grit to earn the title of detective. To discover if we were worthy of the Twinnoggin name."

"Indeed, we did."

"Let us review, shall we?"

"Why not?"

"We were each presented with four challenges to test our mind and mettle. Our moxie."

"That's right."

"Your first challenge to me was to *be normal*. A test of my sincerity. And I passed this test. It was difficult, but I passed."

"You did."

"The second test was to *leave you alone*. A test of my resolve. It was a long week, but this, too, I passed."

"Indeed, you did."

"Your third test provided a greater challenge than those preceding: *to sit on a pole*. A test of my cunning. Did I pass?"

"You sat on a pole, all right. Nobody can dispute that. Your picture was in the paper."

"Indeed, it was. My fourth and final challenge, however, proved the most difficult of all. I was to find out what Hannah really thought of you, but more than that, I was to tell you. To tell you the truth. A truth that hurt. The second part was inestimably more difficult than the first."

"I can see that."

"But I did it."

"You did."

"It was test of my courage, and I passed."

"Indeed."

"Maria, I do believe I have passed the four challenges you set out for me. Do you agree?"

"I do."

"Very well. I am proud to have proven my worth."

"You should be."

"And now we must examine your challenges."

"Indeed."

"My first challenge was a test of your spirit: to zig where others zag. I challenged you to utter the word *rutabaga* in class. And you did. You didn't want to, but you did."

"Rutabaga," I said. It was so easy this time.

"Next, I presented you with a test of your stealth: to place our dear Antonio atop Mr. Zukowski's desk."

"Which I did."

"You passed with flying colors."

"And third?"

"The third challenge was a test of your skills of inquiry.

To determine whether Mom was going to send me to the Academy. You passed once again. By this point, Maria, I was not surprised. By this point I knew you could do anything."

"Thank you."

"As for your fourth challenge…"

"The most difficult of all: I found Cynthia."

JJ paused, drew a breath.

"A fine accomplishment," he said. "One you should be proud of."

"Tell me about it. I just walked three city blocks by myself, for the first time in my life, crossed three streets with no wrong turns, no Maria Pancakes, and then found a speechless autistic nine-year-old girl in a crowded bakery, all without ever seeing her or anything else around me. Oh, and I saved your bacon in the meantime."

"A fine accomplishment, as I said, and one I am grateful for. You showed bravery, intelligence, and resolve, all beyond your years. These are all fine traits, and a must for any detective. But it was not your fourth challenge."

"What?"

"I'm afraid your fourth challenge is still more difficult."

"More difficult than finding Cynthia?" I asked. Right now, right offhand, I couldn't imagine a more difficult day than the one I just had. What did he expect me to do? Cure cancer? Tame a tiger? Hurdle the sun?

"You have done very well, Maria," he said. "You have passed tests of spirit, stealth, and inquiry, and shown remarkable bravery, intelligence, and resolve. But your final test is more difficult still: it is a test of your heart."

"A test of my heart?"

"Indeed."

"What is it?"

"Admit that you're my friend."

38

I Did

And I did.

I did on that day, and the next day, and the day after that when they let me return to school. It wasn't hard, because it was true: JJ was my friend. I didn't care who knew. I hung out at his locker, sat with him at lunch, told all the girls, Hannah especially, that JJ and I were friends. Best friends. Friends for life. It felt good.

I had passed the final challenge. That weekend, JJ formally chartered us as the founding members of the Twinnoggin Detective Agency. It was a strange little ceremony, pure JJ, involving scented candles, Latin incantations, and a rainbow-colored propeller beanie. All I could do was grin.

After the ceremony, JJ announced that we had solved our first case, *The Case of the Missing Sister*. It was an impressive accomplishment, one that required cunning, intelligence, and nerves of steel. We could be proud. But we never took another case. After all we had been through, the petty crimes of Marble City Middle didn't seem nearly so important.

We shuttered the business. We had taken one case—or had it thrust upon us, more like—and we had solved it. The Twinnoggin Detective Agency retired with a 100 percent success rate. Ninety-nine and a half just won't do.

Mr. Torres was alarmed when he heard the story of my solo adventures on Washington Avenue, but deep down I could tell he was proud. I had used my cane and my brain and figured it out. Just what he wanted. We still go out on lessons—there's lots more to learn—but he trusts me more now, keeps an extra step or two behind me. I guess that's what freedom feels like. Or at least the first taste of it.

JJ's mom didn't send him to the Academy, despite her threats. I guess she decided she'd go easy on him this time, seeing as how we had found Cynthia and got her home safely. She said that JJ could stay at Marble City Middle, at least for now. He had such a good friend there in me, after all. *But one more screw-up...*

I was glad to have him there. School was different, *better*, with JJ as my friend. I still paid attention to Hannah and Kaitlyn and the rest, of course. I couldn't not pay attention to them. But what they thought, and what they thought *about me*, mattered less and less every day. That's another kind of freedom, I suppose.

Things at home have changed too. Mom seems more relaxed. Relieved, even. There's a hope in her voice I haven't heard in a while. She's not holding on so tight, and that's a good thing. I'm allowed to go further on my own now, free to walk down Washington Avenue, free to wander the whole neighborhood, free to venture out even further than the bakery, although I rarely do. Most days, I'm either hanging out at home or JJ's. But it's nice to know I could go if I wanted to.

So I'm free now. More free than I've ever been.

Is it all I wanted? Yes and no. Sometimes I miss that closeness, that big smothering motherly embrace of a mom who never wants to ever let me go. A mom who will love and cherish me, and keep me and protect me, no matter what. That's kind of nice, sometimes.

But most times? Most times I'm happy for the freedom, for the trust, for the chance to be who I need to be. I need the space. I need the space to grow and learn and fall and fail, to bump and wobble and conquer and climb. To become who I'm bound to become.

I'm not amazing.
I'm not magic.
I'm just me.
Just Maria.
And that's enough.

ACKNOWLEDGEMENTS

Like a lot of books, *Just Maria* has one author but many sources. I am indebted to all those who helped me find my voice.

As a writer, I wish to thank my advisors past and present, including John Hardwig, Jake Morrill, David Dykes, Stacey Hildenbrand, Ginger & Allan Wolf, and of course my mom, Marilyn Hardwig, who has been my most careful reader for more than forty years. (Is she scribbling Harbrace numbers in the margins of this book? Perhaps.)

Thanks also to my whip-smart editors at Regal House, Jaynie Royal and Pam Van Dyk, who saw something in *Just Maria* and helped it find the light of day.

As a teacher, I give thanks to all those mentors, colleagues, and co-conspirators in Texas, North Carolina, and Colorado, too numerous to mention, who have taught me what I know, and much more that I've forgotten.

Thanks also to IFB Solutions, and in particular Chris Flynt, for sharing the dream, and making the space to dream it. Finally, a big shout-out to my students from across my career, for granting me a steady supply of your insight, energy, and wit. Thank you for sharing your selves, in countless ways. I could not have written this book without you.

As a human, I save my last and biggest thanks for my family, Nita, Eli, and Isabel, for all the years of advice, absurdity, support, and sandwiches; they nourished me then, and nourish me still.